Samuel William Fores, Satirist: Caricatures from the Reform Club

Mark Bills

Published by Gainsborough's House Society
Sudbury, Suffolk, United Kingdom, to accompany the exhibition
Samuel Willam Fores, Satirist: Caricatures from the Reform Club
1 November 2014 – 15 February 2015

Designed by Steve Hayes
Printed by Lamport Gilbert

ISBN 978-0-946511-59-4

Front cover: Henry Kingsbury? (fl.1775–1804), *The Cock of the Walk, Distributing his Favours*, hand-coloured etching, published by S.W. Fores, 31 May 1786 (detail of cat.3)

Back cover: Isaac (1764–1811) and George (1792–1878) Cruikshank, *French Generals Receiving an English Charge*, hand-coloured etching published by S.W. Fores, 28 April 1809 (detail of cat.29)

Contents

Foreword

The Reform Club was founded in 1836, four years after the 'Great' Reform Act finally received a grudging royal assent, having come through a bruising battle royal in Parliament. The Act's principal achievements were the disfranchisement of the so-called 'rotten boroughs' – constituencies that could still send representatives to Westminster, even though they were largely depopulated – and the enfranchisement of the rapidly growing industrial cities. The parliamentary process was accelerated by widespread popular demonstrating and some local rioting, but the country managed to avoid the overwhelming, violent revolution that had shaken France within living memory. A combination of Radical and Whig reformers in Parliament, with Earl Grey as Prime Minister, carried the day against the Duke of Wellington and the Tories.

After their success the reformers commanded enormous popularity, which was reflected in success at the polls. But by setting up an efficient national organisation, with the Carlton Club as its headquarters, the Tories soon began to recover. The reformers took the lesson and established their own political structures, with the Reform Club as their nerve centre. Both clubs were situated, side by side, in Pall Mall.

Caricaturists played a huge role in the propaganda surrounding the debate over reform, with vast numbers of humorous, often vicious cartoons being published, predominantly sympathetic to the reformers' case. Our club's library and archive have accumulated a considerable and varied collection of these, as well as of other political cartoons of those stirring times. Notable among them are 180 caricatures that Samuel William Fores published between 1786 and 1831. This collection represents many of the finest caricaturists of that period and covers a wide range of styles and political and social issues. It is uncertain whether the large album in which the caricatures were kept was acquired by purchase or donation; it most probably arrived in the club after 1894. The album must have been opened very rarely and in consequence the pictures have retained their original colouring in marvellous, pristine condition. In 2002 the Library Committee of the Reform Club decided to have the caricatures detached from the pages of the album and to display them as a group in the clubhouse, thus enabling members to see them for the first time. We are delighted that now, in the context of this path-breaking exhibition and catalogue on the life and work of S.W. Fores at Gainsborough's House, a portion of the Reform Club's collection can be seen and appreciated more widely.

Peter Urbach
Honorary Archivist
Reform Club, September 2014

Acknowledgements

This catalogue could not have been produced without supporters. I am grateful to a number of people and institutions for their help in realising this project. I am most grateful to Mr John Osborn, who at a very early stage chose to encourage the exhibition and catalogue about S.W. Fores and support its realisation. It could not have happened without his support and I am hugely grateful to him. I am also grateful to the Paul Mellon Centre, who support scholarship and help make publications happen, for their assistance in producing this catalogue. The prints in the exhibition are from the Reform Club collection, whose archivist, Peter Urbach, has given much of his time and supported this important loan. Many thanks are due to Mrs Elizabeth Ling, the current owner of the Fores business, and also to Colin Grant for his editing of the text. Finally, scholars such as Sheila O'Connell have provided invaluable advice and help, as have all the staff at Gainsborough's House, particularly Sophie Woods, Julia Smith and Jake Jones. For generosity with their images I am very indebted to the Mary Evans Picture Library, the British Museum and Mrs Ling.

'The Most Complete Collection of Humorous, Political and Satirical Prints' – Samuel William Fores, Satirist

From the late eighteenth century through to the early nineteenth century, when revolt in France led to the rise of Napoleon Bonaparte, English graphic satire flourished. London was the centre of production for singly issued satirical prints, which were disseminated around the globe. Considered a 'golden age' of caricature and satire, it was a period when the works of James Gillray (1756–1815), Thomas Rowlandson (1757–1827), and Isaac (1764–1811) and George (1792–1878) Cruikshank took graphic satire to a new level. At its heart were the printsellers and publishers who commissioned, printed and distributed these images of political, social and personal satire. In particular, three printsellers dominated the market, the triumvirate of Hannah Humphrey (*c.*1745–1818), William Holland (1757–1815) and Samuel William Fores (1761–1838). Although there are numerous studies of the individual artists, there has been no monograph of a producer, yet these figures often pulled the strings, steering the course of a satire and determining its content. The printsellers also ran the business, played to the crowd and patrons, had their own political agendas and chose which artists to patronise.

Of all the printsellers of this period, Samuel William Fores was probably the most prolific; certainly his business had the greatest longevity, surviving until well into the twentieth century and adapting to the market for over two hundred years. Fores worked with all the great satirists of his day and his astonishingly varied output typifies the spirit of satire in its 'golden age'. Through him we are able to discover not only the mechanics of satire and its production but also its impact and use in this seminal period. From the perspective of his entrepreneurial practice, we can see a more complete picture of graphic satire in its heyday.

The growth of the individual print market in London in the late eighteenth and early nineteenth centuries was something of a phenomenon. Directly serving a metropolitan audience, the caricature print trade distributed its productions throughout Europe: one Fores print by Isaac Cruikshank, *French Generals Receiving an English Charge* (1809; cat.29, fig.13), even depicts Napoleon, Talleyrand and other French generals enjoying English caricatures. It was a lucrative business in which Fores was extremely successful and which his descendants were able to continue for many years, adapting to the market as Fores himself had throughout his career. Within his lifetime the nature of satire, particularly its move from individual prints to magazine and journal, changed radically, and the position of caricature – how it was perceived and the strength of its attacks – underwent a complete shift in emphasis.

Always complex, satire encompassed a whole gamut of attitudes: moral, amoral and immoral. It was a business, but it was perceived, and indeed acted, as a scurrilous tool for individual attacks as well as a censor for bad behaviour. In S.W. Fores we can see a mixture of personal and political bias, the publisher reflecting his own views or those of his clients and market interests (something he never lost sight of). In one of the many court cases that he faced for libel, the whole question of satire and caricature was considered by counsel. The target for satire was often articulated at the time as 'human folly', which provided a wealth of material for the satirist: 'It was amusing and instructive to see all the varying shapes and shades of human folly ... It was the lot of human nature not only to increase in wisdom, but to increase in folly also, and as folly increased, the subject of caricature was enlarged.'[1] In this description there is room for entertainment as well as a corrective, exploring bad practice and immorality. Conversely satire could also be seen as a way for 'libellers' to scurrilously and falsely attack individuals by laying 'hold of little infirmities, that had nothing to do with a man's moral character'.[2]

1. Appleton, *Samuel William Fores*, 1825, pastel drawing, private collection.

Fores's own position, like that of most printsellers and publishers, fluctuated. Writers on satire have always been aware of the political bias of his prints, and new evidence of his voting in the Westminster elections confirms that his prints followed his own political viewpoint. It is also clear from his important clients that he did, at times, take up individual causes. We have records, too, of the string of court cases that Fores faced and the evidence that he gave countering libel charges, which throw much light on the world of the caricature printseller. In an advertisement of 2 June 1787 Fores claimed that the object of his productions was 'satire. Its end amusement, instruction and reformation. Through politics, intrigue and fashionable foibles.'[3] With all the inherent contradictions that contained, publicly Fores certainly claimed the moral high ground.

To succeed in this world, Fores was tenacious, resourceful and inventive. Always with an eye to a new opportunity and an enviable list of clients, he occupied a large part of the market. He spotted new talent, working with the greatest satirical artists of the period, including, for example, James Gillray and Thomas Rowlandson from early in their careers. One innovation he introduced was the loan of portfolios of caricatures for the evening. He published a huge number and variety of prints, appealing to most sections of the market. Not many portraits of Fores are known, but a likeness appears in at least one of his prints, *The Tractors* (1802; fig.2), and possibly others (see p.15 and fig.8). A competent pastel portrait (fig.1), dated 1825 and signed 'Appleton', depicts him in profile, the clear features of a central figure of English satire. He married twice, his first wife dying in 1797, and he is known to have fathered sixteen children. Indeed productivity is one of his great claims, as probably the most prolific publisher of singly issued satirical prints in its greatest age and the creator of a business that went from generation to generation.

[1] *The Times*, 17 Feb. 1802, p.3.

[2] *The Times*, 9 May 1800, p.3.

[3] *The Times*, 2 June 1787, p.2.

2. Charles Williams (*fl.*1797–1830), *The Tractors*, hand-coloured etching, published by S.W. Fores, 16 September 1802, British Museum. Fores is shown extracting venom from a scandalmonger, Philip Thicknesse's third wife.

The Piccadilly print shops

Samuel William Fores was born on 8 March 1761 and baptised on the 29th of that month at St Benet Fink, Threadneedle Street, London. His father Samuel Fores (1738–*c.*1800), a member of the Draper's Company, was a stationer and bookseller, based for much of his career at no.120 Strand. At the age of fourteen Samuel William was apprenticed to his father. The indenture, which is dated starting on 12th May 1775, records the standard seven-year period, ending for Fores in 1782. In this year, at the age of twenty-one and with his apprenticeship completed, he had the opportunity of starting his own business. The next year, 1783, was very important for Fores, marked by both his marriage to Elizabeth Green (1758–1797) and his setting up as a printseller specialising in hand-coloured singly issued satirical prints. William Holland, who was to become his main competitor, also started his caricature print business in this year at no.66 Drury Lane, moving in 1786 to no.50 Oxford Street.[4]

The location that Fores selected was at the City Arms, no.3 Piccadilly, near Haymarket (his invoices bear the City of London coat of arms). During the eighteenth century the print business had been moving towards the west of London, from the City along Fleet Street and the Strand to the fashionable West End, and Fores was one of those businesses to begin life

[4] At the end of 1802 he moved to 11 Cockspur Street, where he continued publishing until his death in 1815.

3. Edward Topham (1751–1820), *The Macaroni Print Shop*, hand-coloured etching, published by M. Darly, 14 July 1772, British Museum.

there. His main competitors, Holland and Humphrey, also located to this part of London. Moving to set up his own business was a natural step, but specialising in satire was a change from the kind of book and printselling he had learnt with his father. The reasons for this might have lain in the growing success of the Humphreys at no.18 Old Bond Street, but Fores's model was probably the 'Fun Factory' of Mary and Matthias Darly, which in 1766 moved to premises at no.39 Strand and was famously depicted in *The Macaroni Print Shop* (1772; fig.3). As an apprentice at his father's shop he must have been very aware of this business not far from his workplace at no.120. Here the Darlys showed their caricatures to pedestrians on the Strand, offered drawing lessons and printed designs by amateurs, all strands that Fores would include in his own business.[5] He would have also seen their decline after Mary Darly died in 1780, leaving a gap in the market. His decision to move west was certainly a commercial one, as the market was moving that way.

In her defining catalogue of satire Dorothy George notes: 'Fores, whose imprint first appears in January 1784, comes at once to the front.'[6] The first print that bears Fores's name was

[5] Mary Darly advertised 'materials of every kind used in the Polite Arts of Drawing, Etching, &c with all Sorts of Drawing books for young Ladies and Gentlemen' (*Public Advertiser*, 1 Jan. 1779).

[6] BM Satires, vol.6, p.xxxiii.

4. Anon., *A Beast of Prey / Tally — Tally — Ho*, etching, published by S.W. Fores, 29 January 1784, British Museum.

published on 5 January 1784 and titled *General Blackbeard Wounded at the Battle of Leadenhall* (BM Satires 6367). It was an anti-Fox caricature, drawn by John Boyne, published by Edward Hedges at no.92 Cornhill and, as the print advertised, 'Sold by S. Fores No. 3 Piccadilly'. Operating in the 1780s, Hedges was a family of printers and publishers based in the City of London, and it made commercial sense to sell prints in the West End. It probably means that Fores had begun his business in 1783 by selling other publishers' caricatures, but it was not long before he was publishing his own. *A Beast of Prey / Tally — Tally — Ho* (fig.4), published on 29 January 1784, appears to be the first print he published and is indeed lettered 'First Sketch, published Jany 29 1784 as the act directs, by S. Fores No. 3 Piccadilly'. It is uncertain who drew the image, a crude etching of a bounding fox with the head of Fox on it. It was Tory in bias, anti-Fox at least and a modest start to probably the largest producer of singly issued prints in London and, as such, the world, for London was the centre of this trade.

No.3 Piccadilly remained his address for twelve years.[7] The position of the shop was just opposite the halt of the Paris Diligence, the fast coach that ran daily to the south coast of England to catch the packet boats for the continent. The traffic was both ways and Fores's shop was seen by many visitors and émigrés from mainland Europe, particularly as the troubles in France grew. It was in this shop that he introduced some of his most novel and extraordinary ways in which to attract a market for his prints. Late in 1789 he published *Fores' New Guide for Foreigners, Containing the Most Complete and Accurate Description of the Cities of London and Westminster, and their Environs ... In French and English / Nouveau Guide des Etrangers*, a dual-language guide to London for this market. Reissued in 1790, it could be bought with or without a map (2s extra), 'in which the names of the streets are alphabetically arranged' (title page). Fores stated that his guide was published 'to accommodate foreigners who visit this metropolis', while also affording entertainment 'to the resident man of taste'. It points out the

[7] There are some records of Samuel Fores operating in 1793–4 at no.51 St Paul's Churchyard, which are likely to refer to his father Samuel Fores, as prints by Fores during this period bear the no.3 Piccadilly address (cf. cats 9–11) – unless perhaps he was at St Paul's Churchyard as well as no.3 Piccadilly.

key sites with descriptions in English and French and includes the Bank of England and Chelsea Hospital, as well as places beyond London such as Reigate, Hatfield House and Box Hill. Naturally he takes the opportunity to describe his own shop and what could be seen there: 'To the works of Hogarth, Bunbury, Sayre, and Rowlandson, is added every other Caricature Print, executed by other hands that has been published during the course of many years, the whole forming an entire Caricature History, political and domestic, of past and present Times.' The exhibition of caricatures that he describes, which will be considered shortly, was a characteristic of printsellers at this time, and in a competitive market Fores was emphasising the comprehensive nature of his collection. In the British Museum collection there is a Fores invoice dated 1793 for Lady A. Conally (fig.5), which gives an insight into his clientele at this address and shows that, although specialising in caricature, he sold other prints and related material, in this case ship prints and picture frames for drawings.[8]

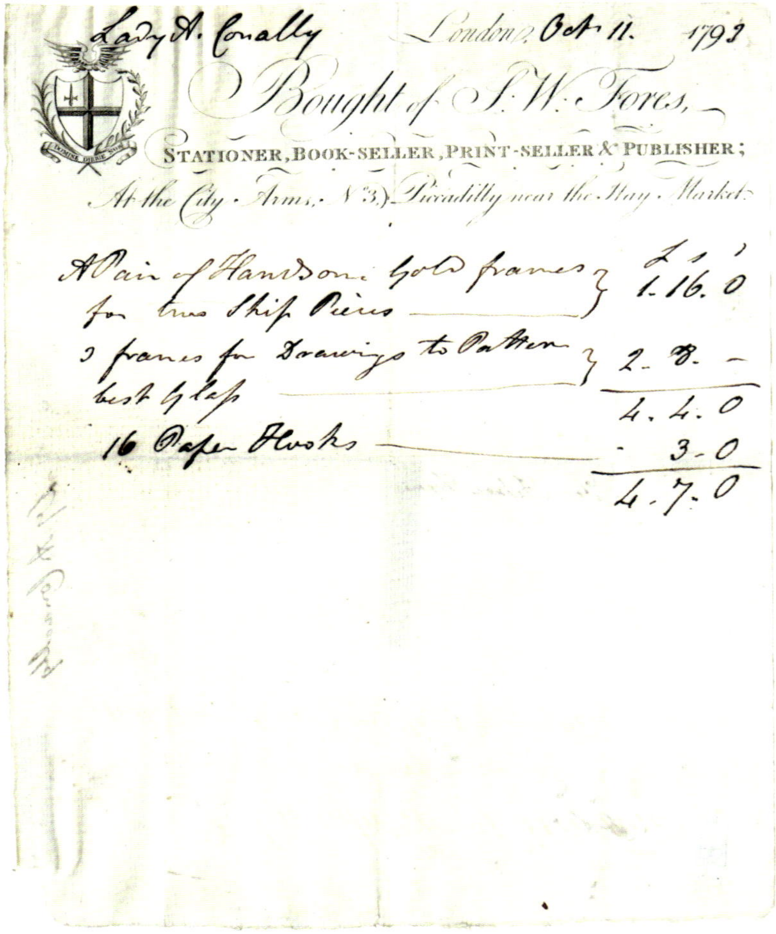
Lady A. Conally London Oct 11. 1793
Bought of S.W. Fores,
STATIONER, BOOK-SELLER, PRINT-SELLER & PUBLISHER;
At the City Arms, No 3, Piccadilly near the Hay Market.
A Pair of Handsome Gold frames for two Ship Prints £ 1. 16. 0
3 frames for Drawings to Pattern best Glass 2. 8. -
4. 4. 0
16 Paper Hooks - 3. 0
4. 7. 0

5. Fores's invoice for Lady Conally, 11 October 1793, British Museum.

We are also fortunate to have an image of the business at no.3 Piccadilly in *The Cock of the Walk, Distributing his Favours* (1786; fig.6, cat.3), and although not topographically correct, it shows that Fores adopted the method of exhibiting to the street by placing his prints facing outwards against each pane of glass. Such displays always attracted attention and often crowds were to be found outside the shop staring at the prints in the window. In this print he attacks the Prince of Wales (something he had been prosecuted for) and makes it clear he is a Tory, showing a partisanship that his fellow printsellers did not do.

Fores's business flourished, and with it came the need to expand and find bigger premises. In 1795 he moved his shop further west up Piccadilly to the corner of Sackville Street, where he remained for the rest of his life. This was at no.50 Piccadilly, although from 1820 it was renumbered no.41. The shop afforded a better position with two front windows, giving him greater visibility, as well as more space to exhibit works. Undoubtedly, too, the premises had an ambience that suited his increasingly impressive client list. Fores had always aggressively marketed his business with exhibitions and sensational objects, but now, through this move, he was going more upmarket and creating something of a fashionable salon, which was fondly

[8] The bill has a letterhead containing a version of the City of London coat of arms with its motto. The printed text reads: 'London / Bought of S.W. Fores, / Stationer, Book-seller, Print-seller & Publisher; / At the City Arms, No.3 Piccadilly near the Hay Market'; and the handwritten: 'Lady A. Conally Oct 11. 1793 / A Pair of Handsome Gold frames for two Ship Prints £1 16s 0d / 3 frames for Drawings to Pattern best Glass £2 8s 0d / [subtotal] £4 4s 0d / 16 Paper Hooks [?] 3s 0d / [total] £4 7s 0d'.

6. Henry Kingsbury? (*fl.*1775–1804), *The Cock of the Walk, Distributing his Favours*, hand-coloured etching, published by S.W. Fores, 31 May 1786 (cat.3). This print depicts Fores's shop front at No.3 Piccadilly.

remembered by those who visited it. The barrister and historian John Adolphus (1768–1845) gave this brief account:

> I remained ... under the care of my great uncle, a widower, living in Sackville Street, then one of the most fashionable localities in town ... My greatest amusement was Fores's caricature shop at the corner of Sackville Street, where in complement with my uncle, I had the privilege of going and turning over all the wonderful caricatures of Rowlandson and Gilray [*sic*]; that shop still remains.[9]

People went to the shop not only to peruse the latest intelligence translated into satire but to meet each other. The Duke of Orléans, Nelson, 'Old Q' (the Duke of Queensbury), Sir Francis Burdett and Sir Arthur Wellesley (the Duke of Wellington) are known to be some of Fores's most notable clients.[10] Memoirs and reports of the shop at no.50 also recount that Fores's second wife, Jane Blucher (1772–1840), was central to this salon: she was well liked by clients and by all accounts a personality who drew people to the shop. Fores's first wife, Elizabeth, had died in 1797, leaving eight children, and he had remarried around 1800.

[9] Emily Henderson (Adolphus's daughter), *Recollections of the Public Career and Private Life of the Late John Adolphus, the Eminent Barrister and Historian: With Extracts from his Diaries*, London 1871, p.3.

[10] Anon. 1912, p.388.

Alexander Broadley's *Napoleon in Caricature, 1795–1821* contains one of the longest accounts of Fores and his Piccadilly salon:

> His second wife Jane helped him look after the shop, and became a great favourite with all the celebrities who made it a trysting-place ... Thither came Sir Francis Burdett (anxious to see the latest picture of his speech from the window of the 'Crown and Anchor'); the young Lord Byron from his rooms, first in St. James's Street and then in the Albany ... General Dumouriez, busy with his plans for the defence of England against Napoleon ... and titled French *émigrés* by the dozen. All these and a great many more congregated at 'Fores's' to chat with the popular lady of the house and laugh heartily at the caricatures, of which they were often the central figure.[11]

One of the émigrés who escaped from France was the Duke of Orléans, Louis-Philippe (1773–1850), who later became King Louis-Philippe. He arrived in England in 1800 and, while in London, stayed in Piccadilly with Fores. According to the Fores family:

> It was in this house [no.50 Piccadilly] that the Duc d'Orleans – afterwards King Louis Philippe – found asylum in the days of his exile, when he was known as 'Mr. Smith,' and it is pleasant to record that the generous hospitality of the original Fores has since been repaid by many graceful acts on the part of the exiled family.[12]

Broadley concurs with this, noting: 'Louis Philippe lived for some time during his first period of exile over the corner-shop.'[13]

Another anecdote to emerge from Fores's famous shop is about one of his most famous clients, Horatio Nelson (1758–1805). Taken from an account by one of Fores's daughters, who remembered him counting out his money with one hand, it is published in different sources and relates to a visit by the admiral in the autumn of 1805, just prior to his death at Trafalgar:

> The great admiral was passing through London on his way to Portsmouth, and called at the print shop to pay his bill, for he had long been a regular customer. Seeing Mrs. Fores in the shop, and noticing that she was likely to soon become a mother, he, with an absence of affectation ... promised to be a godfather.[14]

Although Nelson died shortly afterwards and was unable to fulfil his promise, Jane Fores gave birth later the same year to a boy who was named Horatio Fores in memory of the admiral.[15]

Two of Fores's prints depict the shop at the corner of Sackville Street, *John Bull Guarding the Toy-Shop, or Boney Crying for Some More Play Things* (1803; fig.7) and *Folkstone Strawberries or More Carraway Comfits for Mary Ann* (1810; fig.8). In *John Bull* Fores has his print shop transformed into a toy shop, where Bonaparte, depicted as a petulant child cries over playthings that he cannot have. Symbolically these are the London institutions, including the Bank, India House, the Treasury and the Custom House. The topography of this, like much satire, is specific but not accurately represented, apart from a few details. The railings in front of the

---

[11] Broadley 1911, vol.1, p.58.

[12] Anon. 1912, p.387.

[13] Broadley 1911, vol.1, pp.59–60.

[14] Anon. 1912, p.388.

[15] '"If it's a boy, Mrs. Fores, remember that I should like to be his godfather." Nelson never came back, but the son to which Mrs. Fores subsequently gave birth was duly christened "Horatio Nelson." This story was told to Mr. G.P. Fores by a daughter of the original owner of the shop, who remembered having clung to her mother's side whilst the Admiral counted his money out of a large silken purse, and her having asked her mother where the gentleman's other arm was' (Arthur Irwin Dasent, *Piccadilly in Three Centuries*, London 1920, p.116).

7. Anon., *John Bull Guarding the Toy-Shop, or Boney Crying for Some More Play Things*, published by S.W. Fores, 29 October 1803, British Museum.

print-shop window are an accurate feature: in the late nineteenth century a commentator wrote that this print 'depicts the window of the old shop, with the familiar railings, almost as they exist to-day'.[16] This is significant because the outside of the shop was an important space where crowds would gather to see the latest satires and the railings would have kept viewers away from pressing against the pains of glass but still allowed a clear view. The image is staunchly British, defending the institutions against the French who are shown longing for them through the tearful Napoleon.

Folkstone Strawberries of some seven years later presents a remarkably changed print shop. Drawn by Isaac and George Cruikshank, this finer image shows the exterior and interior of the shop with all the signs of the business's diversification, books taking increasing space from the caricature prints both inside and outside. It has been suggested that Fores is depicted in the interior looking at a ledger on the shop counter. This is possible, but the resemblance to the forty-nine-year-old Fores is not hugely convincing.[17] Outside, the railings, although much changed, and the fan glazing of the door give a good sense of the shop at this time.

[16] Anon. 1912, p.387.

[17] Dorothy George and James Baker, 'The Royal Brat: Making Fun of George Augustus Frederick', in Kremers 2014, p.91. Appleton's portrait of Fores (fig.1) is very different.

8. Isaac (1764–1811) and George (1792–1878) Cruikshank, *Folkstone Strawberries or More Carraway Comfits for Mary Ann*, published by S.W. Fores, 20 June 1810, British Museum.

Fashionable though this part of Piccadilly was, it was not immune to criminal activity and scandal. Several criminal cases are reported relating to the shop at the corner of Piccadilly and Sackville Street. A house painter, whom Fores employed in 1799 to paint the residence, took the opportunity in the course of this work to steal a variety of things, including a large number of caricatures. John Worrall and his accomplice, Susannah Green, were tried at the Old Bailey on 2 December 1799 for the theft from Fores of seventy-seven prints valued at £17, thirty prints valued at 30s and a number of other items. Extraordinarily the printseller searched for the criminals and after more than one attempt finally found them. Giving evidence, Fores recounted that the forty-one-year-old Worrall 'immediately acknowledged he had taken them, and hoped I would forgive him; he never attempted to deny it: I found the diamond and the six prints at the pawnbroker's.'[18] At the end of the trial Worrall was sentenced to death and Green to be transported for seven years.

If robbery was a hazard, most criminal offences relating to print shops such as Fores's were pickpocketing and illegal sexual activity. The crowds around the print-shop windows absorbed in the prints made picking pockets relatively easy. Prostitution was also practised around the lewd displays in caricature shop windows, and gay activity, then illegal, was reported. Two such cases are recorded in relation to Fores's shop at no.41 Piccadilly (previously no.50): the

[18] *Old Bailey Proceedings Online* (www.oldbaileyonline.org), t17991204-39.

9. Richard Newton (1777–1798), *An Exhibition of Caricatures: The Interior of William Holland's Print Shop*, *c.*1794, watercolour, British Museum.

first in 1821 was the charging of Edward Everett with 'gross improprieties with James Baker ... at the caricature shop, the corner of Sackville-street, Piccadilly, on Monday evening between five and six o'clock; also with George Crocker, a lad between 15 and 16 years of age, whom he enticed into the Green-park'.[19]

The case of John Grossett Muirhead in 1825 caused more of a sensation with a packed court of onlookers at the trial. Muirhead was charged with indecent assault, found guilty and sentenced to 15 months' imprisonment and a £500 fine. *The Times* described Fores giving evidence:

> Mr Fores, who keeps a print and caricature shop at the corner of Sackville-street, in Piccadilly, came forward ... He has often observed through his window, as there is generally collected a crowd of persons, the prisoner make his way gradually through them, until he got close to some youth. (Mr. Fores here described the most scandalous practises on the part of the prisoner.) He (witness) having seen repeated instances of this kind of conduct in the prisoner, thought it his duty to consult two magistrates.[20]

Fores claimed he had tried to deter Muirhead by 'holding up to his face a print of the Bishop of Clogher', i.e. Percy Jocelyn (1764–1843), who was the Anglican Bishop of Clogher from 1820 to 1822 and was forced from his position due to claims of homosexual practices. Jocelyn

[19] *The Times*, 31 Oct. 1821, p.3.

[20] *The Times*, 25 Aug. 1825, p.3.

appeared in a number of satires, which presumably Fores sold and one of which he probably held up to his window. Fores claimed that Muirhead was well known and that he had seen him committing his 'practices' for sixteen years. Muirhead spoke out:

> 'And is this you, Mr. Fores,' said the prisoner, 'who comes forward against me – a man whom I have patronized and done material services to?' 'Done me a service,' said Mr. Fores: 'I would not accept a service at the hand of such a wretch. I believe you once laid out 4s or 5s in prints at my shop, if you call that a service.'[21]

Exhibitions and sensations

Between 1786 and 1787 Fores had advertised his shop at no.3 Piccadilly as a caricature warehouse, presumably because it implied a great range of prints at relatively modest cost. Sometime in 1787 he began to simply refer to himself as 'S.W. Fores, Satirist'. In the following year his main rival, William Holland, opened his famous caricature exhibition at no.50 Oxford Street. Claiming that it was the largest collection of humorous prints in Europe, he charged one shilling for the privilege of entering the shop and viewing the exhibition. There was always an audience on the street for the print-shop windows, while the interior attracted a clientele who were more likely to spend. Sadly, only one image has yet come to light of the interior of a caricature shop, that of William Holland, depicted around 1794 in a watercolour by Richard Newton (1777–1798; fig.9). In it every inch of wall space is covered with caricatures, and the room is crowded with the middle classes of all ages from children to the elderly. Opened in 1788, Holland's exhibition was thought to be the first of its kind, but an advertisement placed by Fores in *The Times* of 2 June 1787 states that 'An exhibition of caricatures is this day opened as above', making it clear that Fores had begun such an exhibition around a year earlier.[22] What is less certain is whether Fores charged for entry when he first opened the exhibition or how large the exhibition was, for his early marketing appears somewhat subdued in relation to Holland's bold claims.

Fores was not slow in responding to this and he expanded and marketed his own caricature exhibition in 1789, claiming it to be 'the Compleatest [*sic*] in the Kingdom' and also charging an admission of one shilling. In very obvious competition with Holland, Fores enlarged his own exhibition further, advertising in the same year 'an entire Caricature History, political and domestic, of past and present Times'.[23] In 1790 he reissued *Fores' New Guide for Foreigners* and advertised the exhibition in papers, including *The Times*. The advertisement is interesting in revealing that he had exhibition galleries on two floors of his shop: the ground floor showed paintings and drawings by Old Master artists (demonstrating his diversification) and

> in the above Rooms are the completest Collection of the works of Bunbury, Rowlandson, Sayre, and every artist in Caricature ever exhibited in this Kingdom. Also, a Number of French Caricatures, with the Head and Hand of Count Struenzee. Admission One Shilling. On Friday, will be published a new print ... Price 2s.[24]

---

[21] Ibid.

[22] *The Times*, 2 June 1787, p.2.

[23] Advertisement in *Fores' New Guide for Foreigners ...* , London 1789.

[24] *The Times*, 20 March 1790, p.1, which began: 'Pictures to be Sold Cheap. In Fores's Caricature Exhibition Rooms, No.3, Piccadilly, are deposited for sale, the following pictures at exceedingly low process. A capital Picture of Diana and her Nymphs, Rubens; a Landscape, Claude; a ditto Breughel; a Sea Piece, Ulgen ... Also a Manuscript Missel on Vellum Illuminated &c. Also, Drawings by the following Masters, Corregio, Salvatore Rosa, Titian.'

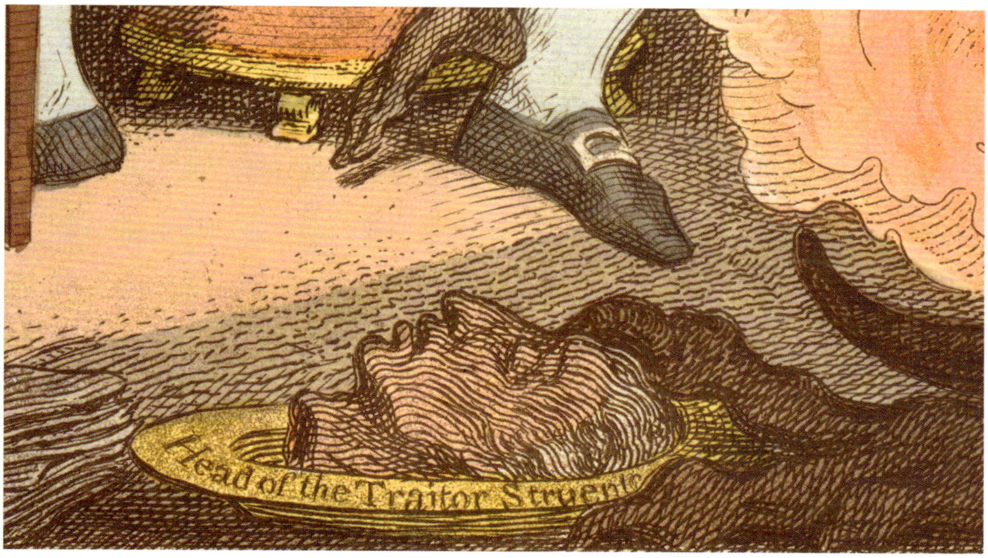

10. James Gillray (1756–1815), *Lieut Goverr Gall-stone, Inspired by Alecto;–or–The Birth of Minerva* (detail), hand-coloured etching, published by H. Humphrey, 15 February 1790, Gainsborough's House. This detail showing Count Struensee's wax head gives an idea of how it might have been displayed in Fores's shop.

Fores also recognised that he had to keep offering something new, and his exhibitions were regularly changed, as is shown by the advertisement on a print dated 20 December 1792 stating that he 'has again opened his Exhibition Room to which he has added several Hundred Old & new Subject[s]'. In 1795 he advertised on a print that he had 'lately fitted up his Caracature Exhibition in an entire Novel Stile admittance one shilling'.

The competition was fierce and Fores realised that, in order for him to put himself ahead of his competitors, he needed something they did not offer. The exhibition and diverse picture stock were common to caricature publishers, so Fores decided to do something sensational. In 1789 *Authentic Elucidation of the History of Counts Struensee and Brandt*, translated from the German by B.H. Latrobe, was published for John Stockdale, opposite Burlington House, Piccadilly, near Fores's shop. It told the romantic and gruesome story of Count Struensee (1737–1773), the physician and reformer in Denmark who had fallen foul of the populace and had an affair with the queen. This had led to his grisly execution on 28 April 1772 when his right hand was cut off before he was decapitated. The story fascinated the public, particularly the affair with Queen Caroline Mathilda, and there was a great revival of interest in the subject fired by the publication of Latrobe's English version of the book. Fores exploited this fascination, as he had access to Struensee's wax death mask and a cast of his hand, which he displayed in his caricature exhibition (fig.10). Not appealing to the best in human nature, it succeeded in drawing in the crowds.

Fores had probably acquired these macabre relics from Philip Thicknesse (1719–1792), with whom he had worked on several occasions, including publishing the first biography of Thomas Gainsborough by Thicknesse in 1788 shortly after the artist's death. In his *New Prose Bath Guide* of 1778 Thicknesse refers to the Struensee casts, which had been exhibited at Shrimpton's Circulating Library, 'each person paying One Shilling'.[25] The guide describes the relics as

> a Cast, taken from the Head and right Hand, of the unfortunate Minister, COUNT STRUENSEE, by Command of the KING of DENMARK, a Piece of Art of so very extraordinary a Nature, that we are justified in saying, from the united Testimonies of some of

[25] Philip Thicknesse, *The New Prose Bath Guide, for the Year 1778*, [London] 1778, p.54.

the best Judges, that, if it is not THE FIRST, it is ONE of the first Pieces of Art in *Europe*. Indeed, it is so perfect a Representation of Death, without any Traces of the Agonies which violent Deaths leave on the Countenance, that, of the many hundred Ladies who have seen it, we do not recollect one, who would not willingly have looked upon it again, nor one who did not think it *too handsome a Head* to be so untimely separated from the Body to which it belonged.[26]

This account was also printed in the *Lady's Magazine* of 1778 (p.312), which indicates that it was purposely marketed to a female audience.

Thicknesse, according to a detractor, James Makittirick Adair (1728–1801), acquired the pieces in Paris. In his *Curious Facts and Anecdotes, Not Contained in the Memoirs of Philip Thickness, Esq.* (1790) Adair notes 'Struenzee's head was not his invention, he purchased it at Paris. This same head has been employed for a variety of purposes. Sometimes a view of it was the condition of selling a pamphlet, sometimes it was a *sixpenny* passport to his *delectable* house and grounds.'[27] Adair also makes it plain that they were a 'waxen figure of the bloody hand and head of count Struenzee'.[28] Fores advertised this curious display in newspapers and at the bottom of his prints, and from this evidence it appears that they were an addition to the exhibition from around June 1790 to May 1793, when he had in place an altogether new attraction.

If Thicknesse's items had been displayed to some effect and drawn a curious public, the next gruesome sensation was to be all the more dramatic. News from France of the September Massacres of 1792 reached London very quickly,[29] and the position of Fores's shop opposite the Paris Diligence meant he was party to new information. The guillotine had been invented in revolutionary France as a humane alternative to more brutal forms of execution, the principle being that it should kill efficiently with as little pain as possible and that it was the same execution for all. It was first used in April 1792 on a highwayman, Nicolas Jacques Pelletier, and was the subject of considerable fascination as a new form of execution in England. This was brought to a height when, on Monday, 21 January 1793, Louis XVI was beheaded by guillotine on the Place de la Révolution, Paris (fig.12). James Gillray's *The Zenith of French Glory; – The Pinnacle of Liberty. Religion, Justice, Loyalty, & all the Bugbears of Unenlightened Minds, Farewell!* (BM Satires 8300), published by Hannah Humphrey on 12 February 1793, was one of the first to give a detailed and accurate depiction of this machine, but Fores bettered this by over a week when on 1 February he published *The Martyrdom of*

DESCRIPTION
OF A
Correct Representation of the GUILLOTINE,
PUBLISHED by S. W. FORES, No. 3, PICCADILLY,
Called, The MARTYRDOM of LOUIS XVI. KING of FRANCE,
With which Print this is given.

THE Axe, near 300lb. Weight, being drawn up by means of a small Windlass affixed to the Side of the Machine, the King was then fastened to a Board, which reached no higher than his Breast, laid along on his Belly, with his Head through the Hole in the Two Boards, (exactly resembling a Pillory); by this Means it is impossible the Sufferer can remove his Head any way. Through the Board that goes over the Neck there is a Cavity to admit the Axe, by which the Head is completely severed in a Moment, and in the Centre of the Neck; the Axe is let go by cutting the Rope, thereby causing no Tremulation in the Sufferer by Noise, the Weight to which the Axe is fixed sliding down with the greatest Velocity, in Grooves cut in the Sides of the Machine. ——See the Companion Plate, called the MARTYR of EQUALITY, representing the Axe down, and the Body laying on the Board, the Duke of Orleans holding by the Hair, the King's Head, to the Populace, exclaiming, "*Behold the Progress of our System!*" And a Grenadier dipping a Handkerchief in the Blood, with the Point of his Bayonet. The above Prints are neatly executed, and sell for 1s. plain, and 1s. 6d. neatly coloured, each.

Also, just published, an admired Song in French and English, set to the Piano Forte and Harp, by Madame Delaval, called *Les Adieux de l'infortunée Louis XVI. à son Peuple.*—The unfortunate Louis XVI.'s Farewell to his People. Price One Shilling.

11. Isaac Cruikshank (1764–1811), *The Martyrdom of Louis XVI. King of France*, hand-coloured etching, published by S.W. Fores, 1 February 1793, and *Description of a Correct Representation of the Guillotine, Published by S. W. Fores, No.3, Piccadilly, Called, The Martyrdom of Louis XVI. King of France, with Which Print This is Given.*

[26] Ibid., pp.53–4.

[27] James Makittirick Adair, *Curious Facts and Anecdotes, Not Contained in the Memoirs of Philip Thickness, Esq.*, London 1790, p.48.

[28] Ibid., p.74.

[29] Reported in *The Times*, 10 and 12 Sept. 1792.

Louis XVI. King of France* (fig.11), drawn by Isaac Cruikshank. Furthermore, Fores accompanied the print with a small publication entitled *Description of a Correct Representation of the Guillotine, Published by S.W. Fores, No.3, Piccadilly, Called, The Martyrdom of Louis XVI. King of France, with Which Print This is Given* (1793).

Fores even went a step further and had a guillotine made for his shop to satisfy the curiosity about it at the height of the executions in France. On his print *False Liberty Rejected or Fraternizing & Equalizing Principles Discarded* (7 March 1793; BM Satires 8311) he advertised 'compleat sets of Caricatures on the French Revolution & … an Exhibition and 1s In the exhibition a Complete Model of the Guillotine'. Fores used contemporary events and especially his intelligence from France to create a sensational history and account of the horrors being played out across the channel. The model of the guillotine was a particular draw and on 8 March he inscribed on a print, *The Last Interview between Louis XVI, King of France, and his Family* (BM Satires 8312), that at his shop 'may be seen a Model of the Guillotine 6 [overwriting '4'] feet high'. Playing on such gruesome interest, Fores sold his depictions of the revolution, which reflected the view of the government and popular opinion.

12. Isaac Cruikshank (1764–1811), *The Martyr of Equality*, hand-coloured etching, published by S.W. Fores, 12 February 1793, British Museum.

Fores marketed his prints in other, less sensational ways. One important method that Fores had at his disposal was the titling of the individual print. Often an amusing pun, the title could tempt a buyer. The reason for this becomes evident when it is remembered that advertising in newspapers and magazines was predominantly text based and so the titles needed to stand out, such as, for example, an advertisement from *The Times* that reads 'BERGAMI PEARS … or Choice Fruit; Which is the Dirtiest?; Oh! My Mother …'[30] According to Broadley, Fores was not averse to writing verse to accompany anonymous prints and cites *Boney and the Gay Lads of Paris Calculating for the Next Triumphant Entry into Moscow* (1813; BM Satires 12033) as an example of this.[31]

As well as advertising in newspapers and inscriptions at the bottom of his prints, Fores used flyers and posters, which were distributed. The British Museum has a flyer advertising the

[30] *The Times*, 9 Oct. 1820, p. 4.

[31] Broadley 1911, vol.1, pp.321–2.

13. Isaac (1764–1811) and George (1792–1878) Cruikshank, *French Generals Receiving an English Charge*, hand-coloured etching, published by S.W. Fores, 28 April 1809 (cat.29).

'Roxburgh Collection of Caricatures' in 1815, which was twenty-four folio volumes available at 250 guineas. Earlier, in 1789, it was also clear that Fores had had cards produced to advertise particularly important prints. Unfortunately these kinds of ephemera are often lost and it is only due to a letter from James Gillray to Fores that we know of one such card Fores made to market a print of Pitt he had commissioned from Gillray (see below, p.26). If advertising took place primarily within the metropolis, there is evidence that distribution reached throughout Europe, as is indicated in *French Generals Receiving an English Charge* (1809; cat.29, fig.13) showing Napoleon and his generals enjoying Fores's prints. Although the butt of the joke was the Duke of York, commander-in-chief of the British army, being mocked by his enemy, the scene was entirely possible, since British caricatures were sold in Europe, as many contemporary European periodicals make clear. Another interesting point about the print is the communal nature of enjoying satirical prints, something that can be appreciated in a group. Sharing a joke is very much part of the enjoyment, and Fores was quick to see the commercial value of this.

From 1793 Fores began to advertise a new attraction at the bottom of his caricatures: lending folios of caricatures out for the evening. *A Tit Bit for the Buggs* (1793; BM Satires 8392) by Thomas Rowlandson included the note, 'Prints & Drawings lent on the Plan of a Circus Library Folios of Caricatures lent out for the Evening'. An advert in *The Times* in February

14. Thomas Rowlandson (1757–1827), *The Caricature Port Folio*, date unknown, watercolour, British Museum

1793 for *The Martyr of Equality* advertised 'Folios of caricatures lent out'.[32] The procedure was that customers paid a deposit and a fee for the loan and, on the safe return of the folio, received their deposit back. Thomas Rowlandson captured the experience in a watercolour now in the British Museum showing a group enjoying a portfolio of caricatures (fig.14). The practice appears to have been popular and continued until the widespread development of illustrated satirical magazines in the early nineteenth century.

Earlier, Fores had started his own periodical, in itself not illustrated, but with a print included. In June 1787 Fores published, advertised and widely distributed *The Plenipotentiary* (no.1, June 1787), stated as 'by a Society of Ladies and Gentlemen'. It was an ambitious idea: a satirical journal that, Fores asserted, aimed to be 'new and multifarious. Its object is satire.'[33] It was to be published in sufficient numbers so that it 'may be purchased in every considerable town in Great Britain, besides in every Bookseller and Printseller's shop in the capital'. It was twenty-four pages of political, social and cultural commentary, and was not particularly exceptional in this regard. What made it different was that 'each number is to be adorned with

[32] *The Times*, 18 Feb. 1793, p.2.

[33] *The Times*, 2 June 1787, p.2.

a striking temporary print, executed by the most eminent caricaturist in town'.[34] The first edition included two prints, and the intention, according to its advertisement, was that it would come out weekly. Only one appears to have been produced and this suggests that either it failed to sell in sufficient numbers, as it was too ambitious and impractical, or that, most likely, only one was ever intended to be published and it was itself a satire of similar journals. Whichever, it only ran to a single issue, and this method of distributing prints, accompanying a pamphlet or magazine publication, was limited to one-offs rather than a sustained series.

The business

In opening a caricature shop in 1784, Fores was not doing something entirely new, as he had been brought up and apprenticed at his father's bookshop and stationers. He had the advantage of knowing the trade and having the contacts, which allowed him to diversify and keep the business lucrative. His sixteen children and a company that survived for over two hundred years are ample evidence of the solid business foundations that he set. Like his father, Fores took on apprentices to work in the shop, such as A.H. Verdier on 24 January 1785 and George Chilcott on 5 April.[35] Also, according to evidence given at a trial, it was stated that in 1802 Fores had a 'shopman', John Herring, who lived on the premises above the shop.[36] Importantly we have indentures for his sons Charles Fores in 1805 and for Henry Philip Fores in 1809, clearly establishing and securing the family business.

What was newer to Fores was the singly issued print, of which he became London's largest producer. His shop at no.3 Piccadilly had two floors of displays. It is likely that his printing presses were on the ground floor and would have consisted of at least one etching press and letterpress, as Fores produced both pamphlets and etchings. The advantage of etching was that it could be a relatively speedy process, as it was for most satire and caricature, which was simple and linear with shading and cross-hatching, plus hand-colouring to further enliven the image. It was particularly useful in responding quickly to news and events before the public lost interest. This is not to undermine the skill of the great satirist who could use line to produce some of the most memorable and significant images of the period. In contrast etching was also a medium that could be used quite easily by amateurs, which, when Fores started his business, was quite important. The Darlys, who had been a model for Fores, regularly produced plates for gentleman amateurs and Fores developed this idea by selling drawing equipment and instructional manuals for budding artists. In a print of 1786, *The Cock of the Walk, Distributing his Favours* (1786; fig.6, cat.3), Fores advertised at the bottom that 'Gentlemen's designs' could be 'executed without any expense'.

It is difficult to calculate how many prints were made from each plate, as the editions were not numbered. Although it is clear that a number were taken from each, after this they were produced in response to demand. Indeed, we know that, when Fores put together folios for sale, many of them were freshly printed, as the hand-colouring appears to have been done at the same time for prints that were created over decades apart. The price of prints to the customer differed according to the sophistication and finish of the print, the quality of the

---

[34] Ibid.

[35] Freedom of the City Admission Papers, 1681–1925, London Metropolitan Archives (online).

[36] *The Times*, 17 Feb. 1802, p.3.

15. John Keyse Sherwin (1751–1790), after Thomas Gainsborough (1727–1788), *The Right Honorable William Pitt*, engraving, published by Robert Wilkinson, 15 June 1789, Gainsborough's House.

paper on which it was printed and whether it was coloured or not. Fores provided a wide range of production quality from the top to the bottom of the market. Prints such as *The Martyr of Equality* (1793; fig.12) and many other singly issued prints of this period cost 1s each when plain, and 1s 6d when 'neatly coloured'.[37] Others that were more complex cost more, some that were crude in execution, less. The expectation was that prints would sell in relatively high numbers in the shop and through distribution. The costs of production for each print necessarily included the fee to the artist who produced the copperplate, the cost of paper (which differed in price and quality), the printing and the hand-colouring; the printing and possibly the hand-colouring took place within the shop. We have an indication of what Fores paid his artists in a letter from James Gillray to the publisher in 1789 when the artist was demanding payment for three plates he had drawn for Fores: 'Ye amount of ye three Plates I will just mention again, as you may have mislaid ye the account – for – Falstaff – 2-2-0 / Pig in a poke – 1-11-6 / Bologna Sausages 2-2-0.'[38] A payment of two guineas for an artist such as Gillray seems to be about standard; for other artists it would presumably be less. The overheads and other production costs meant that the business was based on selling relatively high numbers, which they clearly did, as Fores demonstrated by moving to larger premises in 1795. It is interesting to note that Fores produced a range of prints of variable quality: David Alexander observed in his study of the caricaturist Richard Newton: 'Whereas Holland and other publishers of satires had moved over to using the smoother wove paper, Fores continued to use the rougher and cheaper laid paper.'[39]

Fores dealt with large numbers of prints and produced bound folios for sale as well as for hire for the evening. The Roxburgh Collection of Caricatures of 1815, comprising twenty-four folio volumes available at 250 guineas, has already been noted. There are several accounts of such folios, including that of Henry Angelo, one of the age's finest contemporary commentators on the world of satire, who wrote of Fores: 'I understand he has twenty-five folio volumes of the most choice caricatures of the last and present century, which must be an invaluable *recueil* [compendium], showing not only what we were, but the age we live in.'[40] In

[37] *The Times*, 18 Feb. 1793, p.2.

[38] Gillray to Fores, 5 March 1789, Curzon Collection, Bodleian Library.

[39] Alexander 1998, p.135.

[40] Angelo 1828–30, vol.2, p.294.

June 1800 an MP, Mr Johnes of Hafod, Cardiganshire, ordered from Fores 'all the caricature prints that have ever been published' (see below, pp.34–5).[41]

The amassing of print collections and exhibitions of the history of caricature production reveal Fores's strong passion for and understanding of his business. When it came to employing artists, he worked with the greatest satirists of the 'golden age'. Henry Angelo noted that 'Mr. Fores, of Piccadilly,' has 'many of the very finest drawings executed by Rowlandson in his best days (for latterly they were very inferior)'.[42] His employment of James Gillray in the 1780s (and very briefly in 1791), before he was completely tied to Hannah Humphrey, is significant in Fores's output. An interesting example of their association is Gillray's portrait of William Pitt, which was commissioned by Fores and strained the relationship between artist and publisher.

Fores, a supporter of Pitt, had agreed to the idea of a serious portrait print by Gillray of this great politician, seeing the commercial possibilities of such a project. On 26 June 1788 a contract was drawn up in Gillray's hand and signed and witnessed by both parties. The agreement was that both the profit or the loss was to be equally shared after the deduction of expenses and Fores was to pay Gillray fifteen weekly instalments of 2 guineas. If either of the parties defaulted, a £500 penalty was to be paid to the other. The print was to be taken from a finely worked plate and sold at 15s for an ordinary copy and £1 11s 6d for a proof. Timing was an issue, as it was known that John Keyes Sherwin was preparing an engraving of Pitt after the celebrated portrait by Thomas Gainsborough (fig.15).

Gillray set great store by the print, which he felt would help establish him as a serious artist, and subsequently took a great deal of time over its production. Writing to Fores on 5 January 1789, he communicated his difficulty and irritation at the pressure that Fores was exerting to get it published:

> I find it impossible to get the Plate finished this Month, therefore should imagine the Card which you wish'd engraved & distributed, can be of little use at ye Club ye next Meeting (Thursday next) – as I am certain it will be quite time enough to distribute it ye next meeting after.[43]

The commission was not an entirely happy one and Fores was uncertain about the likeness that clearly had elements of caricature around Pitt's distinctive upturned nose and small chin. Fores also wanted Gillray to continue producing caricatures for him, rather than to focus entirely on this plate. Although undated, Gillray's response dates from around this time:

> The Plate is very forward & I must decline etching the Caricatures that you want – as I have reason to believe that Mr. Pitt will be of more consequence than I at first imagined … With regard to altering ye Nose, Mouth, Hair, Eyes, Chin &c &c &c which you seemed to think unlike, I must observe, that I have had again two opportunities for examining every particular feature of the original – and am convinced that my likeness is a striking one therefore, I will not alter an Iota for any Mans Opinion on Earth.[44]

---

[41] *The Times*, 17 Feb. 1802, p.3.

[42] Angelo 1828–30, vol.2, p.294.

[43] Gillray to Fores, 5 Jan. 1789, New York Public Library.

[44] Gillray to Fores, 1789 (undated), New York Public Library.

16. James Gillray (1756–1815), *The Right Honorable William Pitt*, etching, engraving and stipple, published by S.W. Fores, 20 February 1789, British Museum.

17. James Gillray (1756–1815), *The Right Honorable William Pitt*, etching, engraving and stipple, published by John Harris, 9 April 1789, British Museum.

Gillray completed the portrait and without, it appears from the finished print, altering the face (fig.16). It was published by Fores on 20 February 1789 and was not the success that Fores and Gillray had hoped for. It was widely advertised and distributed, but failed to sell in large numbers.[45] Gillray was unhappy with what he felt was Fores's lack of commitment to the print and produced his own version, which was published on 9 April 1789 by John Harris (fig.17). On 5 March, the day in which *The Times* carried an advertisement for the Fores portrait of Pitt, Gillray wrote to him, effectively ending their business relationship:

> Mr Fores – I should be glad if you would send me word, what day it will be convenient to settle the little account between us, as I am very much in want of ye money, if you cannot spare it just now, if you will send me a note, for the amount at a month from the present time … There is an advertisement, & a print for Mr. Fox for which I am indebted to you. I do not recollect anything beside, if there is, you will deduct it from my bill; ye amount of ye three Plates I will just mention again, as you may have mislaid ye the account …[fig.18][46]

[45] For example, an advertisement in *The Times*, 5 March 1789, p.1.

[46] Gillray to Fores, 5 March 1789, Curzon Collection, Bodleian Library.

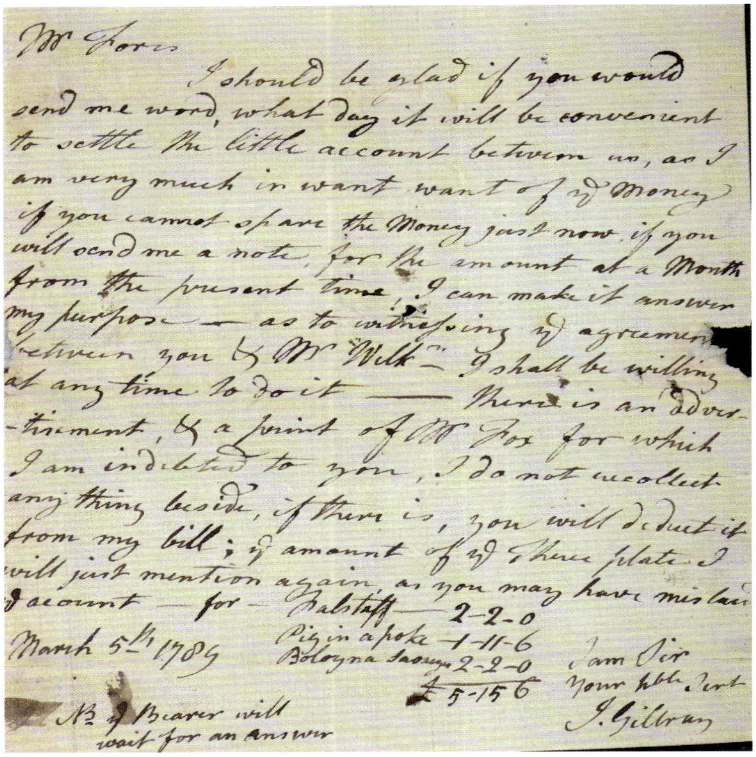

Mr Fores
I should be glad if you would send me word, what day it will be convenient to settle the little account between us, as I am very much in want want of ye Money if you cannot spare the Money just now, if you will send me a note, for the amount at a Month from the present time, I can make it answer my purpose — as to witnessing ye agreement between you & Mr Welk— I shall be willing at any time to do it — there is an advertisement, & a print of Mr Fox for which I am indebted to you, I do not recollect any thing beside, if there is, you will deduct it from my bill; ye amount of ye three plates I will just mention again, as you may have mislaid ye account — for — Falstaff — 2-2-0
Pig in a poke 1-11-6
Bologna Sausage 2-2-0
£ 5-15-6

March 5th 1789

I am Sir
Your hble Sert
J. Gillray

NB ye Bearer will wait for an answer

18. Letter of James Gillray to Samuel Fores, 5 March 1789, Curzon Collection, Bodleian Library, University of Oxford.

19. Henry Kingsbury (*fl.*1775–1804), *The Right Honorable William Pitt*, mezzotint, published by S.W. Fores, 5 July 1789, British Museum.

Fores was equally annoyed with the whole project and chose to publish another serious portrait of Pitt, this time by Henry Kingsbury (*fl.*1775–1804), which was published on 5 July 1789 (fig.19), closely following the Sherwin print after the Gainsborough portrait on 15 June. Fores was also slow in responding to Gillray's demand for payment, and on 19 July Gillray wrote to the publisher once more for the settling of the debt:

> Mr Fores as it is inconvenient for me to engrave any more plates for you, I have sent a bill for those yet unpaid for – I should be glad if you would send word to the Bearer what day this week you chuse to settle ye account
>
> Your hble Sert J. Gillray[47]

Fores did briefly work with Gillray again in 1791, but their fruitful relationship of the 1780s had ended with the Pitt print, which was an ill-judged venture. Fores worked with a number of other leading caricaturists of the period early in their careers, and Thomas Rowlandson has been briefly mentioned. From 1798, however, Rowlandson turned mainly to Rudolph Ackermann for the publication of his prints, even though Fores had been successful in publishing some of Rowlandson's finest images. Fores also worked with the artist Isaac Cruikshank throughout most of his career and later with his sons George and Robert Cruikshank.

[47] Gillray to Fores, 19 July 1789, quoted in Hill 1965, p.33.

Although Fores's main business was caricature prints, the publisher knew all too well the need to diversify in a fickle market. The experience he gained from his father, a stationer and publisher, had taught him about the staples of the trade. The company's longevity was testament to the business's ability to respond to the market. After S.W. Fores's death, when the interest in singly issued caricatures waned, the name became synonymous with sporting prints. Fores did publish small books, but these on the whole were related to his business as a satirist and were mainly in magazine or pamphlet form, often with accompanying prints. A small number were produced with Philip Thicknesse, whose biography of Thomas Gainsborough, *A Sketch of the Life and Paintings of Thomas Gainsborough, Esq.* (cat.38), the first to be written, Fores published shortly after the artist's death in 1788. He produced *Fores' New Guide for Foreigners*, already mentioned, in 1789 and, later, some satirical and political texts such as *The Magic Lantern; or, Green Bag Plot Laid Open; A Poem* [in defence of Queen Caroline] *by a Wild Irish Woman* (1820) and *The Social State of Great Britain and Ireland Considered* (1835) by Thomas Bermingham.

The Piccadilly shops always sold art materials and accompanying manuals for burgeoning artists, and in the 1780s Fores made the offer that 'Gentlemen's designs' could be 'executed without any expense'. Thomas Rowlandson provided instructional drawings for manuals produced by Fores, who in 1790 advertised in *The Times*: 'To All Lovers of Drawing, A new book of outlines of Landscapes and Figures. Etched by Thomas Rowlandson, for the use of Learners, it contains a rich variety of figures suitable to every Design, as well as Landscape, to improve the taste.'[48] These instructional books for amateurs were a good market for Fores, who produced sample drawings for both landscape and figure drawing and painting. In the 1790s Fores published a series of books on drawing the human figure, the fifth volume of which he advertised in 1796: 'No. V of his New Chalk Drawing Book of the Human Figure, from the Features of the Head, through various parts of the body, to a complete Figure, Groupes of Figures, and Historical Compositions, engraved in exact imitation of Chalk.'[49]

Alongside such instruction, Fores sold artists' colours, paper and 'every requisite for Drawing'.[50] For those learning to be an artist, without the benefit of formal training or practising as a professional, these provided practical guides and materials and fed a middle-class interest in artistic production. Drawing masters had long been employed in wealthy families and Fores's trade in materials and instruction benefited from this widening market. The manuals provided a useful guide to drawing skills, but tuition had always included studying and copying the works of other artists. Here Fores saw a further opportunity and offered: 'Fores's Drawing Library, where Prints and Drawings are lent on the plan of a Circulating Library, by the year, quarter, month &c.'[51]

The central position of his shop in Piccadilly gave Fores the opportunity to act as an agent for the various business activities of his clients, particularly those in the provinces who needed a contact in the heart of London. One strand of this was estate agency, where he was the contact for auctions and properties for sale, giving rise to advertisements like that in the guide to Bath by his associate Philip Thicknesse: 'On the 15th June 1789, will be sold by Auction,

---

[48] *The Times*, 12 July 1790, p.4.

[49] *The Times*, 12 March 1796, p.2.

[50] *The Times*, 12 July 1790, p.4.

[51] *The Times*, 12 March 1796, p.2.

ST. CATHERINE's HERMITAGE, near Bath. – For further Particulars, enquire of MR. FORES, Bookseller, in Piccadilly; or of MR. PLURA, Auctioneer, at Bath.'[52] Another area that his business extended into was cultural education. The position of the shop near the Paris Diligence, as well as its reputation, clients and connections, made it a good place to advertise for such business, as indicated by a notice that appeared in *The Times* in 1789 offering language services, training and 'respectable connections' in France. It begins: 'To Parents and Guardians A Middle-aged gentleman, of a small independent fortune, and liberal education, who has resided two years in England, wishes to be the COMPANION or TUTOR to a gentlemen who is desirous to travel into France, or some other part of the continent.'[53]

20. Isaac Cruikshank (1764–1811), *A Man-Mid-Wife*, hand-coloured etching, published by S.W. Fores, 15 June 1793, British Museum.

Advertisements in various publications, like *The Times* and the *Morning Chronicle*, show that Fores also sold items as diverse as general panacea medicines and household paint. The latter is interesting because it was a business in which Fores was a partner. The company, British Wholesome and Cheap Paint Company, founded around 1805, operated from its manufactory at 21 Mary-le-bone street, Golden Square, London. It was claimed that the paint, which was available in 'the most beautiful colours, for the interior of houses … without any unwholesome smell … [and] which will never crack or blister', was used by important aristocratic clients, including the Dukes of Richmond and Norfolk and the Earls Bathurst, Heathfield, Essex and Caernarvon.[54] Made with prepared fish oil, the paint was developed by Fores's partner, a Mr. Vanherman, who 'received a medal and premium from the Society of Arts' for this discovery.[55] Later a further partner joined, and the company, Fores & Mitchell Cheap and Durable Paint, had agents George Moncrieff in Edinburgh and A.M. Fraser in Glasgow.[56] The company was wound up in 1822 when it was announced in the leading newspapers that the partnership had been dissolved.[57]

There is little doubt that Fores had an eye for business opportunity and was willing to branch out into different, but on the whole, related areas. Since he was a dealer, his clients were crucial and what he sold had to be in keeping with his market. Clearly the main thrust of the business was satire, but Fores worked hard to ensure his resilience and sustainability in a rapidly changing market.

---

[52] For an account of Fores's business diversification see *The Print Shop Window ~ Caricature & Visual Satire in the Long Eighteenth Century* at http://theprintshopwindow.wordpress.com

[53] *The Times*, 22 July 1789, p.4.

[54] *The Times*, 28 June 1806, p.3.

[55] Ibid.

[56] *The Glasgow Herald*, 9 Sept. 1814.

[57] For example, *The Times*, 16 Dec. 1822.

Private and public opinion

As a satirist, commissioner, publisher and distributor of satire, Fores was in a position where he necessarily expressed private and public opinion. His social and political caricatures commented directly on the world around him and in so doing took a view. It is interesting to consider whether these views were his own, those of the artists he employed, other figures or indeed the audience whom he needed to attract to increase sales.

In every era there are controversial issues where opinion is split. An interesting example of this was the question of male midwifery, in other words whether men should be allowed to be practising midwives. Many men did practise as midwives, although there was a great outcry against it and Fores was one of those voices. In 1793 he published *Man-midwifery dissected; or, the obstetric family-instructor … In fourteen letters. Addressed to A. Hamilton … Occasioned by certain doctrines contained in his letters to Dr. W. Osborn*. The booklet was by John Blunt, a pseudonym adopted by Fores, and included a satirical print by Isaac Cruikshank of a human figure, half male and half female (fig.20). Fores was against the practice, as each of his letters makes clear. The issue had been debated for some time, and one of the loudest voices against the practice, on the grounds of ill-trained men being allowed such intimacy and causing more discomfort and complications in delivery, was Philip Thicknesse, a long-time associate of Fores, who in 1764 had published *Man-midwifery analysed: and the tendency of that practice detected and exposed*. He died in 1792 and Fores took up his arguments a year later with his own publications. It is difficult to know Fores's motives for pursuing this cause, although presumably he was genuinely against the practice, as well as seeing a market for restating Thicknesse's case and commissioning a print from Isaac Cruikshank. In 1790 Thicknesse was savaged in prints published by Holland and Humphrey (fig.21), which were inspired by enemies of Thicknesse who feared the contents of later volumes of his memoirs and anecdotes. Although Fores did not publish the memoirs, he did sell them at his shop.[58]

21. James Gillray (1756–1815), *Lieut Goverr Gall-stone, Inspired by Alecto;–or–The Birth of Minerva* (detail), hand-coloured etching, published by H. Humphrey, 15 February 1790, Gainsborough's House. Philip Thicknesse is shown with his publications on man-midwifery and Thomas Gainsborough.

[58] 'Proposals for Printing by Subscription in Two Volumes Octavo, Memoirs and Anecdotes of the Life of Philip Thicknesse … Subscribers to pay Half a Guinea with their names, and Half a Guinea on delivery of the second volume … subscriptions received by Mr. Fores bookseller, Piccadilly, and at Meyer's, in the Grove, at Bath' (*The Times*, 1 Dec. 1787, p.1).

Gauging Fores's own opinions can be difficult, but one way in which we can begin to understand them is through his known political views. Most writers of print and satire history rightly surmise that his productions had a Tory bias, which, one might infer, reflected Fores's own position, and fortunately the records of voting in the Westminster elections, in which Fores took part, confirm this view. In 1784 three candidates stood: Samuel Hood (Tory), Charles James Fox (Whig) and Cecil Wray (Whig). Each voter had two votes, which were recorded, and Fores chose to vote for the Tory, Hood (who was elected), and tactically for Wray, avoiding a vote for Fox. In 1788 Hood stood again, this time against one candidate, Thomas Townshend (Whig), and each voter cast one vote, which for Fores was again Hood, although this time Hood was not successful. In this election Hannah Humphrey was paid by Pitt for anti-Whig propaganda, whereas Fores was not. Gillray's biographer, Draper Hill, notes: 'Possibly Fores drew the line at party propaganda; it is more likely that he wasn't asked.'[59] It may also be that he already showed a Tory bias, so it was not considered necessary for him to be paid. Hill does gives us the example of Fores paying Gillray to attack Warren Hastings (1732–1818), who gave a 101-carat diamond to the king without mentioning it was actually a gift from Nizam Ali Khan (1734–1803; see cat.6).[60] We have one more record of Fores voting, which showed a change in his politics; it was near the end of his life in 1837, when three candidates stood: George DeLacy Evans (Liberal), John Temple Leader (Liberal) and George Murray (Conservative). Fores voted for Evans and Leader, and Leader was elected.

Fores was a very strong voice in relation to the events in France with the revolution and the rise of Bonaparte. In this respect his prints adopted the government's stance of hostility and war against the Republic. He was vociferously opposed to Fox and his support for aspects of the revolution and for peace with France. This found expression in prints such as Isaac Cruikshank's *Peace Offering to the Genius of Liberty and Equality* (1794; cat.10). The rise and fall of Napoleon received detailed coverage in his satires, and Fores fashioned himself as 'Caricaturist to the First Consul'. In fact Fores was possibly the first to caricature Bonaparte: *Buonaparte at Rome Giving Audience in State*, 12 March 1797 (BM Satires 8997), by Isaac Cruikshank is an early depiction of Napoleon.[61] His enjoyment of writing titles and verses for the caricatures he produced found full expression in his prints against Bonaparte:

> No! No! Mister Nap, you'll not feather yor cap
> Any more, for your race is near run;
> And your murderous heart is destined Bonaparte,
> To suffer for crimes it has done.[62]

In later life Fores formed a friendship with the political writer and publisher William Hone (1780–1842), and two letters of correspondence exist between the two (Adelphi University, Garden City, New York). Sadly, the letters, which date from 1820 and 1821, do not give us much information about either men's thoughts, but display the mutual respect and friendship of colleagues.[63]

---

[59] Hill 1965, p.31.

[60] Hill 1965, p.30.

[61] See Broadley 1911, p.98: Fores was the first English publisher to print a caricature against Napoleon.

[62] Penultimate verse of a poem below the print, *Boney and the Gay Lads of Paris Calculating for the Next Triumphant Entry into Moscow* (1813; BM Satires 12033).

[63] William Hone Collection, Special Collections, Adelphi University Libraries, Garden City, NY.

Libel, morality and controversy

Prosecuting for a libel in satirical prints was a difficult business, although they obviously contained specific targets. If the king, government or person of station chose to object to a print and seek prosecution, a very clear-cut case had to be made. The majority of cases brought against publishers or indeed individual artists for singly issued caricatures were unsuccessful. Seditious texts were an entirely different matter, but the ambiguity of the image and the dissociation inherent in allegory and exaggeration meant that such cases were difficult to prove, even though the majority of viewers knew who the target was meant to be.

In his career Fores faced several prosecutions about his satirical productions and on one occasion prosecuted an MP who had refused payment due to the alleged offensive nature of his prints. On 24 April 1786 Justice Hyde served a warrant on Fores for selling a print 'supposed to allude to the Prince of Wales and Mrs. Fitzherbert', about which the newspaper further reported:[64]

> The prosecution is supposed to commence from Carlton-House, as Mr. Weltjee has the entire direction, the justices refusing and delaying to take any steps till he came to the office. Several conversations have been held with Mr. Fores previous to his being served with a warrant respecting the print; one particularly with Mr. Smith, in Duke-street, St. James's, the brother of Mrs. Fitzherbert, to whom Mr. Fores obligingly offered to do everything in his power to stop the sale of it.

There is no further news of the prosecution, which probably means that it was dropped. Fores's own response was to publish a print on 31 May, *The Cock of the Walk, Distributing his Favours* (1786; fig.6, cat.3), which flaunted the prosecution. The subject is the Prince of Wales, who is referred to throughout the print, including as a spurred game-cock, but is not represented directly. This is set against the backdrop of Fores's shop at no.3 Piccadilly, where the windows openly display prints alluding to Mrs Fitzherbert and the Prince of Wales, each of which could be the one for which he faced prosecution.

A decade later, in 1796, Fores was one of several printmakers arrested in relation to a print by James Gillray published by Hannah Humphrey on 9 January that year. The print, *The Presentation – or – The Wise Mens Offering* (BM Satires 8779), depicted Fox and Richard Sheridan paying homage to the baby Princess Charlotte, who had been born two days earlier. As with the earlier print, *The Cock of the Walk*, Fores was arrested, this time along with Gillray and other printsellers. Fores's arrest was reported along with other Bow Street crimes, where he faced the magistrate W. Addington, Esq:

> Mr Fores the proprietor of a print-shop in Piccadilly, was on Friday taken into custody, on a warrant offered against him … wherein he stands charged with contemptuously and impiously exposing to public sale a certain print, entitled, 'The Presentation, or the Wise Men's Offering', which is considered … as a burlesque on the scripture picture of the Wise Men's Offering to our Saviour, but is supposed to relate to a recent event at Carleton House. The offence being proved, by the production of one of the prints, purchased at Mr. Fores shop, he was ordered to find bail to answer the complaint at the next sessions for Westminster.[65]

---

[64] *The Times*, 29 April 1786.

[65] *Caledonian Mercury*, 28 Jan. 1796.

The print was relatively inoffensive and the incident a storm in a teacup. Fores was released on bail and the matter taken no further.

Not every action against Fores was prompted by criticism of royalty, and on one occasion, in 1800, he found himself prosecuted at the Court of the King's Bench after producing a caricature with the purpose 'to ridicule the present system of Education of Surgeons in the Hospitals of London'.[66] Although the print is currently unidentified, it is described as showing two gentlemen surgeons visiting a man in the last agonies of dying at St Bartholomew's Hospital and was apparently the work of a student. The dying man in the print was a Mr Bartholomichi, a dancer at the Opera House, who in fighting against being arrested for debt was beaten and received a fatal blow on the inside of his mouth with a poker. This rather gruesome event, which took place on 15 March, was reported in the newspapers and John Wilson was tried for his murder at the Old Bailey, but found not guilty on 28 May.[67] The caricature was produced some time in the second half of March and appeared at the King's Bench on 8 May. The basis of King versus Fores was that the print depicted two respectable individuals of social standing, the surgeons Mr Long and Mr Earl, who had attended the dying man at St Bartholomew's Hospital. The work had caused grievance to the individuals concerned, but Thomas Erskine (1750–1823), who led the case, used it for a wider discussion of the damaging effect of caricature and asked for a rule to show if there was any reason why Fores should not be allowed to be prosecuted, because 'this system of libelling by Caricature Prints, was becoming but too prevalent, and was too seldom made the subject of legal animadversion'.[68] He also observed that caricatures were now carried about (possibly a reference to Fores's folios being lent out) and 'exhibited in different places for amusement'. The judge, Lord Kenyon, sympathised with Erskine and was 'extremely glad the motion was made!' On 14 May the ruling was made absolute, as no cause was shown why Fores might not face a criminal prosecution, although it does not appear to be reported and the case seems to have been dropped or settled out of court.[69]

The most infamous case in which Fores was directly involved was that against Thomas Johnes (1748–1816), the Welsh MP, agriculturist, translator and collector, in 1802. It appears that in June 1800 Johnes had given an order to Fores 'for a complete collection, of all the [satirical] prints that were ever published'.[70] On 27 December in the same year he wrote to Fores asking about the progress of the collection. Fores responded asking about the details of the size of folios and whether the complete works of Rowlandson and Bunbury should be included. He received no reply, so continued to put together the collection, writing again to Johnes saying the prints were ready for delivery. On 4 May 1801 Johnes wrote to Fores saying that he wished the printseller to halt the formation of the collection. In June 1801 Fores delivered the collection to Johnes's seat in Wales. The total cost of the collection was £137 10s, which gives an indication of how many prints there were. If the average plain print was around 1s and a coloured one, 1½–2s, and we know that the total sum was not subject to discount, the size of the collection would be around 1,500 prints, a very large number. No payment was received for the prints despite several demands, so Fores took action.

---

[66] *The Times*, 9 May 1800, p.3.

[67] *Old Bailey Proceedings Online* (www.oldbaileyonline.org), t18000528-39.

[68] *The Times*, 9 May 1800, p.3.

[69] *The Times*, 15 May 1800, p.3.

[70] *Morning Post and Gazetteer*, 17 Feb. 1802.

This time Fores was the plaintiff, as he took Johnes to court, and this time he had Thomas Erskine representing him. The trial took place on 16 February 1802 at the King's Bench with the judge, Mr Justice Lawrence, presiding. Erskine was amusing as he explained the narrative of events, comparing them to a set of Hogarthian satirical prints that might be called an 'AMATEUR'S PROGRESS', from Plate 1 where the amateur orders the prints to Plate 5 where the jury awards the plaintiff £1,000 in costs and damages, with the defendant cursing. The box of prints in question was 'one of the chief sources of amusement during the trial': a caricature of Erskine appeared in the prints that were to be circulated, but it was immediately put to one side and not handed around.[71]

Johnes's defence has been of great interest in the history of satire. His refusal to pay for the prints was on the grounds that the order had been countermanded and on the content and quality of the prints, described by Johnes as 'trash'. He claimed that the collection included duplicates and triplicates of 'common' prints and those of an 'obscene and immoral' nature. The advice of Mr Justice Lawrence was that Johnes should not pay for any prints that 'shocked decency' and that the identification of these was better decided between the parties rather than by a jury looking at and deciding for over 1,000 prints, which would have been most interesting, if somewhat time consuming.[72]

This was not Fores's last time in court, as on 26 July 1824 he appeared as a defendant on copyright charges. The likenesses of the infamous murderer John Thurtell and his accomplices, Joseph Hunt and William Probert, were taken from drawings at the trial in December 1823 and made into engravings. The exclusivity of the prints was important to the publisher in order to be profitable, but soon after their production they were copied and widely sold. Fores was one of those who sold the copied prints and was prosecuted along with the other sellers. He admitted that he had sold the print, but in ignorance, and that when he learnt that it was an illicit copy, he had stopped selling it. The jury found in favour of the plaintiff, who was awarded £50.[73]

Legacy

Samuel William Fores died on 3 February 1838 and was buried in the Fores family vault at St James's, Piccadilly. The business continued to be run by his sons, George Thomas Fores (1806–1858) and Arthur Blücher Fores (1814–1883). Fores had always understood the need to adapt to the market, and as singly issued satirical prints began to be eclipsed by comic magazines and journals, the firm turned to sporting prints, which are still produced today. A watercolour in the British Museum by Thomas Hosmer Shepherd (1793–1864) shows Fores's shop as it was in 1853, the railings still visible (fig.22).

Fores's print production from 1783 to 1838 spanned the 'golden age' of satire of the late eighteenth and early nineteenth centuries. His significance in its development, as probably the most prolific publisher of caricature prints of this period, was immense. His history provides further illumination of the nature of visual satire in Georgian England, of how and why they were produced and of the varied markets to which Fores responded so well. As the

---

[71] Ibid.

[72] Ibid.

[73] *The Times*, 27 July 1824, p.3.

commissioner of prints, a salesman and a commercial gallery director, Fores had a variety of motivations. Undoubtedly a prime incentive was to make money and a strong commercial sense underlies much of his activity, particularly in the diversification of his business into a number of related, but different areas.

22. Thomas Hosmer Shepherd (1793–1864), *Sackville Street, the Longest Street in London without a Turning,* 1853, watercolour, British Museum. This shows Fores's famous shop at the corner of Sackville Street and Piccadilly.

One of the roles of Fores's prints was to provide moral censure, to condemn folly and shine a light on the foibles of others. Attacking people's follies, one might think, was potentially dangerous and Fores did at times sail very close to the wind. He knew, however, how far he could go and was always prepared to back down and stop selling a particular image if litigation threatened. In contrast to his attack on individuals, Fores was very careful about public opinion and the market, of which he needed to be acutely aware. And if you could escape prosecution because of the ambiguity of the visual image and of allegory, that did not mean that it could not be commonly understood. His customers and public opinion did not need to prove anything in court, which could just turn against you, particularly if it didn't agree with the sentiment of the print. Printsellers had to be very careful about this and there is no doubt that Fores played to popular prejudice. This does not mean that he went against his own convictions, his anti-Fox feelings, for example. It is interesting to note, however, that in 1790, when a number of satires by various publishers attacked his associate Philip Thicknesse, Fores joined in with a print possibly by Thomas Rowlandson, *Philip Quarrel the English Hermit and*

Beaufidelle the Mischievous She Monkey, Famous for her Skill on the Viol de Gamba (1790; BM Satires 7724). Less vitriolic than most, such as James Gillray's *Lieut Goverr Gall-Stone, Inspired by Alecto* published by Hannah Humphrey (1790; fig.21), it did perhaps illustrate an example of putting public opinion above personal loyalty.

A significant aspect of satire, and one for which Fores makes an exceptionally good case study, is the way in which it transferred news and information to an interested public. When Fores published a description and image of the guillotine, and then made a model, it had never been seen in England before and he knew that it would draw crowds. No doubt Fores presented it as a horrific artefact of the terror in Paris, an implement of torture, even though the guillotine was intended to be revolutionary and more humane than previous methods of executions in France. It was used as the same punishment for all, whatever their social rank or the nature of the capital offence. In his position opposite the Paris Diligence, Fores had good intelligence about what was happening in France and was able to use satire to attract and inform his customers.

When Henry Angelo reflected on Fores's collection of satire, he realised that it showed 'not only what we were, but the age we live in'.[74] As social history, Fores's immense production is invaluable, presenting the immediate and sometimes visceral responses to events and individuals, revealing loves and hates, hopes and fears. Fores epitomises the prolific and dynamic printseller, reflecting and distorting to expose motives in the confusion of the world around him.

---

[74] Angelo 1828–30, vol.2, p.294.

Catalogue

This is the catalogue of an exhibition held at Gainsborough's House from November 2014 until February 2015. It consists of a selection of prints published by Samuel William Fores between 1786 and 1830. They all come from a folio volume held in the Reform Club, Pall Mall, but were put together by Fores, and as such are a fascinating insight into his output and the folios he compiled for clients.

The WAPPING CONCERT.
MADAM MARY informs her Friends & the Public in General, that she has opened her Winter Concert at the HOG in ARMOUR WAPPING, in a large Commodious room belonging to the Free Masons; as she has at a great Expence, Engaged the best Performers its needless to repeat how very inferior H——r S——e Music meetings must be to hers; after assuring the Public Sig.r Bladder Bridge, Mynheer Van Jews Trump, Sig.r Salt Box, Joe Evans, the celebrated Drummer, with others of equal note will assist in the band, there can be no doubt her Concert will be the Admiration of all Europe Madam M— begs her Polite Audience will excuse her sitting during the Performance, as she contracted in her infancy a Disorder called Le Genoue Inflexible, or (Stiff Knee) which prevents her Standing, even in the most Sacred Pieces of Music — her Enemies call it Pride, but must appear only Malice, when she could not rise before their Majesties, or at the Sacred Name of Jehovah.
Publish'd Feb.y 26th 1786, by S. W. Fores, at the Caricature Warehouse, N.o 3, Piccadilly.

1.

Henry Wigstead (*c.*1745–1800)

The Wapping Concert

Lettered: 'Publish'd Feby 28th 1786, by S.W. Fores, at the Caracature Warehouse, No.3 Piccadilly'

Etching and aquatint (hand-coloured impression), 296 x 332 mm

Literature: BM Satires 7067 ('attributed to Wigstead by Mr. Hawkins'); Michael Burden, 'Mara, Gertrud Elisabeth (1749–1833)', *Oxford Dictionary of National Biography*, Oxford University Press, 2004: online edn, May 2006

This rather crude and cruel satire was aimed at the German singer Gertrud Elizabeth Mara (née Schmeling, 1749–1833), who had found disfavour with the British public in the mid-1780s. Although her debut in London in 1784 was a triumph, receiving the recognition of the Prince of Wales, in the following year several incidents inflamed public opinion against her. Despite initial success in the roles that she sang, which were widely praised, she was seen as haughty and disrespectful, compounded in the eyes of the British by being foreign.

On Wednesday 22 June she performed at Oxford to great applause until she refused to give an encore, causing a 'hiss of disapprobation' (*The Times*, 2 July 1785, p.3). The following night there was an even greater stir during a performance when she '*indecently* sat down when every other principal performer stood up' (*The Times*, 2 July 1785, p.3). She promised to stand during the Hallelujah and Amen choruses of Handel's *Messiah* but did not, incensing the audience further, so that on Friday the 24th she was greeted with 'Off! Off!' from the audience, who would not let her sing. Her later public apology about her ill health was treated with scepticism and she continued to attract bad press for setting up her own subscription concerts, in opposition to those already established in London, and employing predominantly foreign players: 'Madame Mara's establishing a Subscription Concert on her own account, displays a conspicuous proof of her *benevolent gratitude*, for it has already transpired that her orchestra is not to contain one *Englishman* (*The Times*, 2 Nov. 1785, p.2).'

Fores's print of 1786 sets the scene of Madame Mara's subscription concert in a Masonic Hall in Wapping. The accompanying text below refers to her snubbing of the concerts in Hanover Square, her use of foreign musicians and, most of all, her refusal to stand during parts of performances:

> Madam Mary informs her Friends & the Public in General, that she has opened her Winter Concert at the Hog in Armour Wapping belonging to the Free Masons; as she has at a great Expence, Engaged the best Performers its needless to repeat how very inferior H—r S—e [Hanover Square] Music meetings must be to hers … Madam M— begs her Polite Audience will excuse her sitting during the Performance, as she contracted in her infancy a Disorder called Le Genoue Inflexible, or (Stiff Knee) which prevents her Standing, even in the most Sacred Pieces of Music – her Enemies call it Pride, but must appear only Malice.

Certainly, the singer suffered from rickets in her childhood, but it is uncertain how this affected her in later life. The satire also mocks the ritual and appendages of Freemasonry and has Madame Mara perform seated, singing in a heavy foreign accent Fielding's famous song, 'Oh the roast Beef of Old England', to a low audience in poor surroundings.

2.

Henry Kingsbury? (*fl.*1775–1804)

The Royal Academy

Lettered: 'Published 13th April 1786, by S. W. Fores at the Caricature Warehouse, No.3, Piccadilly'

Hand-coloured etching, 284 x 377 mm

Literature: BM Satires 6944

The Royal Academy depicts the Prince of Wales being taught the art of boxing by George Hanger, 4th Baron Coleraine (1751–1824). Hanger, an army officer, writer, beau and clubman, was a rakish companion of the prince. Considered one of the dissolute influences on the prince, he indulged in gambling, racing and pugilism. Here the Royal Academy, rather than displaying the elevated arts, gives way to boxing. The art on the walls depicts scenes of violence, including duelling and the classical Dying Gladiator. The Prince of Wales stands in the middle with his coat on the chair, while Hanger to the left receives instruction from the man to their right.

This is a companion print to *The Royal Society* (11 April 1786), which similarly explores the inappropriately indulgent behaviour of the Prince of Wales and his dissipated companions, including George Hanger.

THE ROYAL ACADEMY.
Published 13th April 1786, by S. W. Fores, at the Caricature Warehouse, No. 3, Piccadilly.

PARTRIGE
Purveyor of Geese to His Highness &c
FORES
Purveyor of Caricatures to the Public No 3 Piccadilly
BULLOCK
Purveyor of Meat to His Highness &c &c
THE COCK of the WALK, DISTRIBUTING HIS FAVOURS.
Published May 31, 1786 by S W Fores at the Caricature Warehouse No 3 Piccadilly
NB Gentlemens Designs Executed without any Expence

3.

Henry Kingsbury? (*fl.*1775–1804)

The Cock of the Walk, Distributing his Favours

Lettered: 'Published May 31, 1786 by SW Fores at the Caracature Warehouse No.3 Piccadilly'

Hand-coloured etching, 289 x 392 mm

Literature: BM Satires 6961

This is an important print in the history of Samuel Fores, being one of the few surviving images of Fores's print shop at No.3 Piccadilly. It is probably by Henry Kingsbury, whose surname is written on one of the copies held at the British Museum, and was printed shortly after Fores's prosecution for 'selling a print supposed to allude to the Prince of Wales and Mrs. Fitzherbert' (*The Times*, 29 April 1786, p.3). This is indicated in the lettering, which includes 'Prosecution Invt – Justice fecit', an adaptation of the standard Latin terms used on prints to mean 'Prosecution created [painted] – Justice made [engraved]'. Clearly responding to this, Fores has the Prince of Wales referred to throughout the print, although he is not represented directly, just symbolically as a spurred game-cock.

The insignia of the Prince of Wales's feathers can be found in the beak of the cock, who has lost them from his tail. They are also shown as bunches of flowers in a wheelbarrow and inscribed to various ladies, including Mrs Fitzherbert. The barrow is being drawn by Louis Weltje (1745–1810), Comptroller to the Prince of Wales, who was heavily involved in the prosecution of Fores, and the contents are being arranged by George Hanger, 4th Baron Coleraine (1751–1824). The three-feathered crest can also be seen on the shops on either side of Fores's: a poulterer's shop to the left inscribed 'Partrige Purveyer of Geese to His Highness &c' and to the right 'Bullock Purveyer of Meat to His Highness &c &c'.

The setting is Piccadilly, although not topographically correct, with Fores's print shop, 'Purveyer of Caracatures to the Public No 3 Piccadilly', in the centre, which, instead of bearing three feathers, bears three heads on spikes representing Charles James Fox (1749–1806), Edmund Burke (1729–1797) and Frederick North (1732–1792). There are nine panes of glass on either side of the door where Fores's prints are displayed to pedestrians of Piccadilly. These defiantly show prints alluding to Mrs Fitzherbert and the Prince of Wales and include *The Royal Toast: Fat, Fair and Forty* (1786; BM Satires 6927), *Out of Fits, or the Recovery to the Satisfaction of all Parties* (1786; BM Satires 8253) and *The Follies of a Day or the Marriage of Figaro* (1786; BM Satires 6924).

4.

James Gillray (1756–1815)

Foul Play, or Humphreys and Johnson a Match for Mendoza

Lettered: 'Pubd Jany 18th 1788 by S.W. Fores. No.3 Piccadilly'

Hand-coloured etching, 199 x 328 mm

The great satirist, James Gillray, worked on a number of prints for Fores in the 1780s and then briefly in 1791, carrying out commissions for satires as well as serious subjects. This sporting print was drawn by Gillray for Fores to commemorate the first contest between the two great pugilists, Richard Humphries (*c.*1760–1827) and Daniel Mendoza (1765?–1836), towards the end of the eighteenth century. The men met at Odiham in Hampshire on 9 January 1788 after an enormous build-up in the press. This is one of several prints at the time that recorded their famous encounter. Accounts of the contest differ, and despite Humphries being declared the winner, all agreed that the result was far from decisive and a further meeting was fixed. They met again twice, near Stilton, Cambridgeshire, in 1789 and finally in Doncaster, South Yorkshire, in 1790, and Mendoza won both contests.

The match at Odiham was full of incident, and although Mendoza gained an early advantage, he withdrew after nearly half an hour due to injury. This print focuses on the question of whether there was 'foul play' on behalf of Humphries by his second, Tom Johnson (real name: Thomas Jackling, *c.*1750–97). A rough, former prizefighter, Johnson berated Mendoza throughout the match, stopped Humphries from falling and, according to the print, even stepped in to deflect a blow, changing the momentum of the contest. The incident is graphically recorded in this image, and a lengthy description of the turning point of the fight is scratched below it:

> Dedicated to Wilson Braddyl Esqr. Gymnastico Generalissimo. This extraordinary Match was Fought at Odiham in Hampshire Jany. 9th. 1788, after 25 Minutes Contest, Mendoza by his superior Skill carrying off the Honors of the day from his Antagonist, when Johnson after having recovered Humphries (who was nearly deprived of Life from a Knock-down Blow) by pouring cold water on his Stomach, finding him still weak & staggering from another blow, & Mendoza aiming another which must have decided the Battle very Judicously steped [*sic*] in between, & by his address entirely chang'd the Scene; in consequence of which, several Gentlemen (who did not wish to gain by collusion) withdrew their Betts. Humphrey relying on such another Step, has thought proper to accept Mendoza's Challenge for another Combat, but like a bold Briton! has proposed such terms as he knows his antagonist cannot possibly comply with from the state of his finances!!! — 'I have done the Jew!' [...] see Humphries Letter to Braddyl.

Price 1s.
TRING.
HUMPHRIES.
JOHNSON.
MENDOZA.
JACOBS.
ISAACS.
ALLEN. MORAVIA
FOUL PLAY, or HUMPHREYS and JOHNSON a Match for MENDOZA; Dedicated to Wilson Braddyl Esqr. Gymnastico Generalissimo.
This extraordinary Match was Fought at Odiham, in Hampshire Janr. 9th 1788. after 25 Minutes Contest, Mendoza by his superior Skill carrying off the Honors of the day from his Antagonist, when Johnson after having recovered Humphries (who was nearly deprived of Life from a Knock-down Blow) by pouring cold Water on his Stomach, finding him still weak & staggering from another blow. & Mendoza aiming another which must have decided the Battle very Judiciously steped in, between, & by his address entirely changd the Scene; in consequence of which, several Gentlemen (who did not wish to gain by collusion) withdrew their Betts. Humphrey relying on such another Step, has thought proper to accept Mendoza's Challenge for another Combat. but like a bold Briton! has proposed such terms as he knows his antagonist cannot possibly comply with from the state of his finances!!! —— "I have done the Jew." see Humphries Letter to Braddyl.
Pubd. Janr. 18th 1788 by S. W. Fores. No. 3 Piccadilly

5.

Henry Kingsbury (*fl.*1775–1804)

A Cotilion

Lettered: 'Pub June the 1 1788 by S W Fores No.3 Piccadilly'

Etching, 215 x 2105 mm

Literature: BM Satires 7441; Gaston Vuillier, *History of Dancing*, London 1898, p.427 (part repr.)

A French dance, the cotillion was introduced to Britain in the eighteenth century when it became all the rage. Dancing masters offered lessons in how to best perform it and the Prince of Wales was an enthusiast. Gaston Vuillier in his history of dance (p.429) describes the trend:

> In their eighteenth century Cotillions the lady dancers accordingly appeared in short skirts, with their overdresses picturesquely looped up, as may be observed in all the diversified pictures of this popular Round … Frequent references to the Cotillions danced at public entertainments in the eighteenth century, and attesting their popularity, are found in the journals and magazines of the time; their vogue extended from country assemblies … to Court balls.

This long etching, printed on four separate sheets joined together (detail reproduced here), depicts ten couples performing the dance with varying degrees of success and visual incongruity. Such designs were made popular by Henry Bunbury (1750–1811) and this one is based directly on his engraving *Long Minuet* (1787). Later Fores republished Bunbury's plate of the *Long Minuet* and others in the series from 1787 to 1794.

6.

Henry Kingsbury? (*fl.*1775–1804)

Les Folies á la Mode

Lettered: 'Pub July 29 1788 by S W Fores No 3 Piccadilly'

Hand-coloured etching, 349 x 485 mm

Literature: BM Satires 7359

This satire is the right half of a large print, whose left half is captioned *Fashionable Follies*. The print consists of a series of vignettes arranged in two strips and depicts anonymous and well-known figures from the highest echelons of society, and their follies.

Here, on the top row, we see a barber at court kneeling before a lady. In the middle the figure named 'Malice la Malice' is Edward Thurlow, 1st Baron Thurlow (1731–1806), who is cutting his throat after seeing in the newspaper the 'Appointment of Sr Pepper Arden'. His opposition to the appointment of Richard Pepper Arden, 1st Baron of Alvanley (1745–1804), as Master of the Rolls was notorious. The last scene of the top row, 'Correction á la Francoise', depicts the Prince of Wales kneeling humbly at the feet of the Duke of Orléans (a client of Fores), who stands above him flourishing a whip.

The bottom row shows George Hanger, 4th Baron Coleraine (1751–1824; see cat.2), with a pistol in his mouth and a piece of paper protruding from his pocket that reads 'Debts of Honr'. The next two, 'Comedy La Comedie' and 'Cat Eating / Le Mangeur de chats', portray silly theatricals. The final pair, captioned 'Diamond finding / Trouvaille de Diamant', shows Queen Charlotte stooping to pick up a diamond, while the king looks on, saying, 'put it in your Pocket'. This is a reference to the supposed bribery of Warren Hastings (1732–1818), who gave a 101-carat diamond to the king without mentioning it was actually a gift of Nizam Ali Khan (1734–1803).

7.

Isaac Cruikshank (1764–1811)

How to Gain a Compleat Victory, and Say, You Got Safe out of the Enemy's Reach

Lettered: 'Pub Decr 15 1791 by S W Fores No 3 Piccadilly'

Hand-coloured etching, 243 x 350 mm

Literature: BM Satires 7932

This satire depicts an imagined scene from the Third Anglo–Mysore War (1789–92), a conflict in southern India between the Kingdom of Mysore and the East India Company and its allies, which included the Maratha empire and the Nizam of Hyderabad. It is one of many that depict Charles Cornwallis, 1st Marquess Cornwallis KG (1738–1805), retreating from Seringapatam in May 1791. From 1789 to 1792 Cornwallis led British and Company forces to defeat the ruler of Mysore, Tipu Sultan (1750–1799). The campaign eventually succeeded with the siege of Seringapatam in February 1792 and a treaty signed in March of that year.

The setback in 1791 at the beginning of the monsoon season was satirised by a number of artists, including James Gillray in *The Coming-On of the Monsoons; or The Retreat from Seringapatam*, published on 6 December 1791 by Hannah Humphrey (BM Satires 7929). Cruikshank's image depicts Tipu Sultan on his horse lifting his bottom and excreting over Cornwallis, who is seated on an elephant. Raising a sabre above his head, Cornwallis cries: 'These Monsoons are more Violent / than ever I knew them before / Boy turn back again.'

8.

George M. Woodward (1760?–1809), designer; Isaac Cruikshank (1764–1811), etcher

A Long String of Resolutions for a New Year

Lettered: 'Pub. January 2, 1792, by S.W. Fores, N. 3 Piccadilly'

Hand-coloured etching with some stipple, sheet of 4 prints, *c.*330 x 520 mm each

This is a long print (detail shown here) in which sixteen individuals amusingly illustrate the various follies of human nature, from vanity to self-delusion. Despite being created for an audience in the late eighteenth century, the targets are very recognisable to a contemporary audience. These include a fearsome bullying woman with a cudgel, who is 'Resolv'd to be meek no longer'; a poor, bad poet, who is 'Resolv'd to indulge the World with no more works of Genius till better paid for them'; a gossip, who is 'Resolv'd to bid farewell to Scandal'; a glutton with gout, who is 'Resolv'd to live very abstemious'; a drunk, who is 'Resolv'd not to drink so much in the future'; and a confirmed bachelor, who is 'Resolv'd to live Single'.

Evacuation of Holland and Brabant or Evacuation de la hollande et du Brabant

9.

Isaac Cruikshank? (1764–1811)

Evacuation of Holland and Brabant or Evacuation de la Hollande et du Brabant [*A Dose for Dumourier*]

Lettered: 'Pub April 11 1793 by S. W Fores No.3 Piccadilly Where may be seen a Modle of the Guillotine 6 feet high also the Head and Hand of Count Struensee Admittance one Shilling'

Hand-coloured etching, 256 x 388 mm

Literature: BM Satires 8322

On 1 February 1793 revolutionary France declared war against Great Britain and Holland. One of the first actions following the declaration was for General Charles-Francois Dumouriez (1739–1823) to invade Dutch Flanders and Zeeland. He was driven back at Neerwinden on 18 March, and this satire depicting the retreat shows Dumouriez vomiting and urinating as he flees the Austrian army led by the Count of Clerfayt. An Austrian officer holds a large syringe bearing Clerfayt's name. In the foreground a woman, the spirit of liberty, lies dead on the ground, the cap of liberty snapped in two.

Dumouriez later defected and became an adviser to the British government. During his time in England he became one of Fores's clients, as Broadley (1911, vol.1, p.58) describes:

> General Dumouriez, busy with his plans for the defence of England against Napoleon … And titled French *émigrés* by the dozen. All these and a great many more congregated at 'Fores's' to chat with the popular lady of the house and laugh heartily at the caricatures, of which they were often the central figure.

10.

Isaac Cruikshank (1764–1811)

A Peace Offering to the Genius of Liberty and Equality / Dedicated to those Lovers of French Freedom Who Would thus Debase their Country

Lettered: 'Publ Feby 10 1794 by SW Fores No 3 Piccadilly'

Hand-coloured etching, 265 x 385 mm

Literature: BM Satires 8426

On 21 January 1794 a new session of Parliament opened with a debate on the war with France. Fox and Sheridan spoke for peace, Fox concluding 'by proposing the following amendment: "To state to his Majesty the determination of the House to support the honour and independence of the Crown – but to advise his Majesty, to consent to a peace on such terms as may appear to be prudent and advantageous"' (*The Times*, 7 Feb. 1794, p.3). To a Tory such as Fores this seemed like kowtowing to a corrupt and bloody regime, which was the main thrust of this satire with its visceral and crude misrepresentation of Fox's and Sheridan's position. To the right is a monstrous symbol of the French Republic sat astride barrels of gin. At her feet lies a decapitated woman who is the figure of justice beheaded and with her sword and scales fallen from her hands.

A group made up of members of the Opposition make the journey to France donning revolutionary *bonnets rouges*. They are from the front (right to left): Charles Stanhope, 3rd Earl Stanhope (1753–1816), carrying an image of the House of Lords and offering a Bible, sceptre and crown, while a mitre falls from his hand; Richard Brinsley Butler Sheridan (1751–1816), with 'The Bank' on his head; Charles James Fox (1749–1806), the most prominent as leader of the Opposition, carrying 'India House' and the royal arms, from which the British Lion is departing in disgust; Samuel Whitbread (1720–1796), following with barrels from his brewery on his head; Francis Russell, 5th Duke of Bedford (1765–1802), with a staff; and finally Thomas Erskine, 1st Baron Erskine (1750–1823), carrying a pile of books on his head named 'Treason \ Law of \ Libel \ Misprison of [Treason]'.

The British Delegates Respectful application for Peace
India House
The Bank
House of Lords
Murder
Famine
atheism
Rapine
GIN
REPUBLIC
HOLLANDS GIN
GIN
GIN
A PEACE OFFERING To the Genius of LIBERTY and EQUALITY.
Dedicated to those Lovers of French Freedom who would thus Debase their Country

An OLD MAID in search of a FLEA.

On record Bold FLEA with Columbus youll stand,
Who sought the American shore,
Like him you undaunted explored a new Land.
Where MAN never venturd before !!

11.

George M. Woodward (1760?–1809), designer; Thomas Rowlandson (1757–1827), etcher

An Old Maid in Search of a Flea

Lettered: 'Published by S W Fores No 3 Piccadilly Septr 25 1794'

Hand-coloured etching, 350 x 230 mm

Literature: BM Satires 8535; Joseph Grego, *Rowlandson the Caricaturist*, London 1880, vol.1, pp.320, 324

This is a companion print to one published by Fores four months earlier, titled *A Tit Bit for the Bugs* (25 May 1793; BM Satires 8392). The common theme of pests appears in both, bed bugs plaguing a fat man in the first and fleas infesting an old maid here. The discomfort of the biting fleas is very apparent and the old woman's rigorous search for them is emphasised by the concentration on her face and the position of her body. A verse at the bottom adds humour to the image:

On record Bold Flea with Columbus youll stand,
Who sought the American shore,
Like him you undaunted explored a new Land
Where MAN never ventured before!!

12.

Isaac Cruikshank (1764–1811)

Suffolk Rats Protecting their Cheese or the County Fencibles Called to Arms

Lettered: 'Pubd Jany 1st 1795 by S W Fores No 3 Piccadilly'

Hand-coloured etching, 248 x 352 mm

Literature: BM Satires 8597

On 1 February 1793 revolutionary France declared war on Britain, raising the question as to whether Britain was sufficiently prepared for such a threat. As a response many companies of men were raised throughout the land, including 'fencibles' (from 'defencible') drawn from the counties. These volunteer forces acquired nicknames including the 'Essex calves' and 'Hampshire hogs.' The 'Suffolk rats' were raised in October 1794 and saw action in Ireland in the Rebellion of 1798.

Fores's print of 1 January 1795 takes the nickname of the Suffolk fencibles, depicting them literally as rats defending an enormous cheese. A sign proclaims: 'Wanted a number of stout able Bodied young Men for the Suffolk Fencibles &c enquire at the Sign of the Hard Cheese.' A large cat in the left of the print is being violently repelled by the uniformed rats under the banner of 'To honor we call you not press you like slaves'. Several satires were produced at this time on Britain's volunteer forces, which were being raised voluntarily rather than, as the satire implies, by force in France.

London Pub. Jan.y 1st 1795 by S W Fores No 3 Piccadilly who has lately fitted up his Exhibition in an Entire Novel Stile admittance one Shilling
TO HONOR WE CALL YOU NOT PRESS YOU LIKE SLAVES
HARD Cheese
wanted a number of stout able Bodied young men for the Suffolk Fencibles &c enquire at the Sign of the Hard Cheese
SADDLES To LET
Suffolk Rats protecting their Cheese or the County Fencibles called to Arms

London Pub: January 7 1795 by S.W. Fores N 3 Piccadelly
My Dear General you have well Executed your Commission; but could not you prevail on any of the Polish Women to POISON their Husbands?
Go my little Ariel & prepare our Altars for these pretty Sacrifices, we must have te Deum on the Occasion
thus my Royal Mistress have I fulfill'd in the fullest extent your Tender Affectionate & Maternal Commission to those Deluded People of Poland, & have here brought you the Pickings of Ten Thousand Heads tenderly detached from thier deluded bodies the Day after Capitulation
Bravo this out does the Poison Scene
ROYAL RECREATION

13.

Isaac Cruikshank (1764–1811)

Royal Recreation

Lettered: 'London Pub: January 7 1795 by S W Fores N 3 Piccadilly'

Hand-coloured etching, 240 x 357 mm

Literature: BM Satires 8607

On 23 December 1794 *The Times* published the 'Particulars of the Storming of Praga, and of the Surrender of Warsaw'. The article (p.4) reported the horrific events of the besieging and capture of the Polish capital, particularly in the area of Praga, a suburb of Warsaw:

> In the assault of the suburbs of Praga … [General Suvoroff] enjoined his soldiers to give quarter to no one. This engagement … will be numbered amongst those which human blood was shed in most abundance, even in these unhappy times in which we live. The number of unfortunate Poles, who perished by the sword, the fire, and the water … are estimated … in the suburb of Praga [as] 12,000 inhabitants of both sexes, and all ages … [They] were the victims of the full fury of the Russians, who massacred all whom they met, without distinction of age, sex, or quality.

This satire is a direct response to the horrific events that took place in Praga in November 1794. Cruikshank's etching is set at the Russian court with Empress Catherine II seated on a throne and receiving decapitated heads from General Suvorov. The general offers the gift of the heads, saying: 'Thus my Royal Mistress have I fulfilled in the fullest extent your Tender Affectionate & Maternal Commission to those Deluded People of Poland, & have brought you the Pickings of Ten Thousand Heads tenderly detached from their deluded bodies the Day after Capitulation.' In response the empress replies: 'My Dear General you have well Executed your Commission.' In fact, Suvorov was rewarded by the empress with the rank of field marshal and a gift of jewels.

14.

Isaac Cruikshank (1764–1811)

The First Articles in Requisition at Amsterdam or the Sans Culotts Become Touts Culotts

Lettered: 'London Pub Jany-29 1795 by S W Fores No 3 Piccadilly'

Hand-coloured etching, 253 x 399 mm

Literature: BM Satires 8613

In January 1795 the French revolutionary army of sans-culottes entered Amsterdam without resistance. Pillaging was forbidden, although the army sorely needed clothes and provisions. The use of 'assignats' (paper money issued by the French National Assembly from 1789 to 1796) alongside requisitioning caused general discontent.

This satire depicts the sans-culottes in Amsterdam requisitioning the trousers of the Dutch. The skinny French are engulfed by the roomy pantaloons of the portly Dutch. A Dutchman, now without trousers, is dismayed: 'Oh my Dollars & Ducats D—n their Citizenship; A fellow here calls me Frere Citoyen and takes away all my Property.' A ragged but happy Frenchman in outsized Dutch breeches, wearing a *bonnet rouge* and dancing with joy as he holds a bottle of Holland gin to his mouth, says: 'They may talk of the Coldness of this Country but by Gar here is the Warm Liqour for De inside & de Warm breeches for de out side.' Coins pour from the breeches, and it is clear that the Dutch are being robbed by the French.

They may talk of the Coldness of this Country but by Gar here is de Warm Liquour for De inside & de Warm breeches fo de out side.
Oh my Dollers & Ducats. D—n their Citizenship; A fellow here calls me Frere Citoyen and takes away all my Property.
Aye, Aye Equality is the order of the Day ça Liberte, for the Carmagnoles
I don't like this Equality
these Plundering Fellows here, I suppose they'll
make use of my Frow next.
DOLLARS for the use of the National Convention
London Pub Jan. 29. 1795 by S W Fores No 3 Piccadilly
The first ARTICLES in REQUISITION at AMSTERDAM or the SANS Culotts become touts Culotts.

NO GUINEA PIGS
Just enter'd holy orders, eh!!! a Snug living Damme!!!
No, I'll wear my own Amber Tresses. A Dirty fellow to Tax us fair Creatures.
Now for a Pleasant Promenade
How I was admired in Hyde Park on Sunday!!
Put flour in my Head. Make a Dumpling of it, eh?
Have you Seen my Belly?
Have you seen my Jaeey.
I don't quite like these Carroty Locks of mine but I'll not be a Guinea Pig, no no.
No Guinea Pigs light Welch Wool, no Dumpling Dust.
What a Helegant Valking Dress for a Citizens Vife.
By Jane what strange sort of Outlandish Creatures we be.
Now I think we have done the Minister; we'll teach him to meddle with Maidens hair.
The TOWN BEFORE YOU, or WELCH WIGS, or WHIMSICALLITIES, or how to Save the Tax on HAIR POWDER.

15.

Artist unknown

No Guinea Pigs / The Town Before you, or Welch Wigs, or Whimsicalities, or How to Save the Tax on Hair Powder

Lettered: 'Pubd March 17 1795 by S.W.Fores No 3 Piccadilly'

Hand-coloured etching, 427 x 537 mm

In 1786 William Pitt had imposed a tax on hair powder, and on 5 May 1795 a new levy was introduced taxing the wearers of the powder the sum of a guinea. Hair powder was still fashionable at the time, especially on wigs, and it was aimed to raise around £200,000 a year with the new tax. It covered those who sported modish pigtails, leading the Opposition to call it the 'guinea pig' tax and those who used hair powder 'guinea pigs'. Many who opposed the tax had their hair cropped or did not apply powder. There were certain exceptions to the tax such as clergymen (with an income of under £100), privates in the army, naval officers below commander, yeomanry, and volunteers (*The Times*, 7 May 1795, p.3).

In this caricature Fores shows us twelve amusing ways of avoiding the new tax. Published just two days after it became law, it suggests that the main way to escape the levy was through ludicrous clothing, although the first character has 'just entered the holy orders' to avoid it, saying it is 'a snug living Damme!!!'

16.

George M. Woodward (1760?–1809), designer; Isaac Cruikshank (1764–1811), etcher

A New Dutch Exercise

Lettered: 'Pubd April 1st 1795 by S. W. Fores No 3 Piccadilly'

Hand-coloured etching, 349 x 487 mm

Literature: BM Satires 8633

Revolutionary France had declared war against Great Britain and Holland on 1 February 1793, and in 1794–5 France successfully invaded Holland, which capitulated, the Dutch people rallying to the revolutionary cause. City after city was occupied by the French, and on 19 January, after William V had fled to Britain, the Batavian Republic was proclaimed (it lasted until 5 June 1806). As the revolution expanded, Britain feared for its own security.

Woodward's print depicts eight fat and lazy Hollanders in two rows and rebukes them for putting up such little resistance against the French. The first figure is a Dutch soldier fast asleep with a gin bottle and musket at his feet, while the words above him proclaim: 'Watch with Diligence!!' The third figure with his back to the viewer carries the text: 'Face your Enemies!!' Another Dutch soldier drops his muskets and runs. All in all, the Hollanders are represented as fat, stupid, lazy and cowardly, appealing to a British audience alarmed at how easily France had overrun Holland.

Watch with Diligence!!
Advance with Spirit!!
Face your Enemies!!
Stand to your Guns!!
Reverence Treaties!!
Afsist your Government!!
Obey your orders!!
Rise in a Mafs!!
A NEW DUTCH EXERCISE.

17.

George M. Woodward (1760?–1809), designer; William Hanlon (*fl.*1795), etcher

Licenced to Wear the Breeches / Did you Ever See Such a Fool as my Wife has Made of me?

Lettered: 'Pub. June 1, 1795 by SW. Fores No 3 Piccadilly'

Hand-coloured etching, 298 x 231 mm

Literature: BM Satires 8760

This print is a companion to *Licenc'd to Wear Hair Powder* (cat.18), which was published on the same day, by the same artists and following the same format. In contrast to the chimney sweep, here is a more affluent fat man who is equally ludicrously dressed, in this case obeying his wife's dictate to follow fashion, as the subtitle makes clear. The tight jacket, the smothered neck and the ridiculously high waist, makes the man look like a Russian doll. The manicured dog to the right and the ribbon that hangs from his waist emphasise the effeminate fashion for a man whose face, cudgel and outspread hands show how out of place he feels with it.

18.

George M. Woodward (1760?–1809), designer; William Hanlon (*fl.*1795), etcher

Licenc'd to Wear Hair Powder

Lettered: 'Pub. June 1 1795 by SW. Fores 50 Piccadilly corner of Sackville Street'

Hand-coloured etching, 290 x 220 mm

The companion print to cat.17, this is another satire that mocks the hair-powder tax introduced on 5 May 1795 (see cat. 15). Clearly the one-guinea tax, which led to those paying it being referred to as 'guinea pigs', could not be afforded by many, including chimney sweeps. Here we see the ludicrousness of a chimney sweep black with soot and sporting a sculpted white wig full of hair powder. The humorous contrast of black and white was also found in eighteenth-century May Day celebrations that featured a chimney sweep and a milkmaid together, as depicted in Francis Hayman's *The Milkmaid's Garland, or Humours of May Day* (1741–2; V&A). In the nineteenth century there was a further tradition where the sweep was covered in flour and the miller in soot.

A SCARE—CROW.
Pub. July 11th 1796 by S.W. Fores 50 Corner Sackville St Piccadilly

19.

William Hanlon (*fl.*1795)

A Scare-Crow

Lettered: 'Pub. July 11 1795 by S.W.Fores 50 Corner Sackville Street Piccadilly'

Hand-coloured etching, 352 x 248 mm

Literature: BM Satires 8759

A Scare-Crow is a caricature depicting a thin elderly woman bedecked in the most inappropriately fashionable clothes that jar with her age and frame. Its title compares her to a ragged country mannequin designed to scare birds. She is wearing a large turban with massive ostrich feathers, and a huge black-brush aigrette, her hair just visible below her neck and armpits. She holds a giant fan in her right hand, and a heavy chain with an oval medallion hangs from her neck. The sleeves of her dress hug her skinny arms, and the high waist almost reaches her neck, presenting her as at once shrivelled and exuberant.

20.

Isaac Cruikshank (1764–1811)

The Political Locust

Lettered: 'Pubd August 14 1795 by S W Fores No 50 Piccadilly the Corner of Sackvill St'

Hand-coloured etching, 271 x 360 mm

Literature: BM Satires 8672

The year 1795 was difficult for Britain, facing war, food shortages, an unstable economy and uncertain future. Cruikshank depicts the state of the nation with the Prime Minister Pitt as a giant locust sitting on the island-fortress of 'Poor Old England' and beginning to nibble a withered tree that bears the inscription, 'The Remains of the Old Constitution'. England is depicted as an isolated island with its battlements bearing the names of its troubles: 'War, Excessive Taxes, Foreign Loans, Subsidies, Guarantees, Treachery of Allies, Monopoly, Dearth of Pros, Civel Discord, Unprincipal Opposition, Extrovigant Pr[ic]es, Professed Atheism amongs[t] the Great, Immense Debt.'

To the left of his head a swarm of locusts are arriving in England representing 'French priests', the destitute clergy who were finding refuge in England. With military setbacks and changing allegiances across Europe, England felt in a vulnerable position, isolated and under siege. In this print Pitt, a devouring monster, says: 'I must take care of my self & my own Relations.'

21.

William Hanlon (*fl.*1795)

The State Caterpillar

Lettered: 'Pub. by S. W. Fores 50 Piccadilly 1 Sepr 1795'

Hand-coloured etching, 274 x 436 mm

Literature: BM Satires 8676

Pitt is depicted as the head of a caterpillar, a chrysalis and a butterfly. The metamorphic process begins with the central image of a giant 'State Caterpillar', Pitt's head nibbling leaves that read 'England, Scotland, Ireland'. The state is represented through Pitt, literally the head of state, with sections of the body representing offices of state: 'First Lord, Chancellor, Constable, Warden, Keeper, Admiral, Commissioner, Master, Governor, High Steward, Places, Pensions, Sinecures, Reversions, Hereditaments, Expectations &c, &c, &c.' Like Cruikshank's representation of Pitt as a giant locust (cat.20), this print also expresses through a striking zoomorphic image the difficulties that Britain faced in 1795.

In the caterpillar's metamorphosis Pitt emerges from the chrysalis over Holland, his closed eyes turned away from the country that had conceded so easily to revolutionary France. In the final phase, as a butterfly, Pitt looks down at France malevolently, his aggression emphasised by the upturned barbed tail.

A New Way of POSTING a LIBEL

Pub Nov 23 1795 by S W Fores No 50 Piccadilly the Corner of Sackville Street _ Folios of Caracatures lent out for the Evening

22.

Unknown artist

A New Way of Posting a Libel

Lettered: 'Pub Novr 23 1795 by S W Fores No 50 Piccadilly the Corner of Sackville Street'

Hand-coloured etching, 346 x 237 mm

Literature: BM Satires 8694

On 13 November 1795 the *True Briton* carried a letter offering £500 reward 'for a paltry libel upon the whole race of Grenvilles', apparently written by George Nugent-Temple-Grenville, 1st Marquess of Buckingham (1753–1813). The letter was, according to its supposed author, an 'impudent forgery … which I would not have given 5 farthings to have kept out of every newspaper' (Dropmore Papers, quoted in BM Satires 8694).

This satire depicts George Nugent-Temple-Grenville posting a bill offering 'Five Hundred Pounds Reward'. His bag makes clear his identity by showing the family coat of arms with the Temple motto, 'Templa quam dilecta' (how lovely are thy temples), a pun on the surname and on the family's large number of garden 'temples'. A speech balloon reads: 'There it is in capitals, – the Libel at full length, and five hundred pounds reward – he that runs may read, I think I shall be a match for the Ghost!!' Presumably this means that Grenville is posting a libel in response to the ghostwriter. Certainly libel is the subject of this satire, Fores himself being prosecuted for it on several occasions.

23.

Isaac Cruikshank (1764–1811)

A Fashionable Information for Ladies in the Country

Lettered: 'Pub Decr 9. 1795 by S W Fores No 50 Piccadilly the Corner of Sackville Street'

Hand-coloured etching, 339 x 230 mm

Literature: BM Satires 8758

This satire was based on the fashion of simple lines that defined the figure or, as the subtitle states: 'The present fashion is the most easy and graceful imaginable – it is simply this – The petticoat is tied around the neck and the arms put through the pocket-holes!!!' The extravagant turban with two feathers, the shoes, and the watches that hang from her neck serve to highlight the smock-like simplicity of the dress itself. The title, *A Fashionable Information for Ladies in the Country*, suggests that the style, with its very makeshift look, might be easily created in the country.

A FASHIONABLE INFORMATION for Ladies in the Country
The present fashion is the most easy and graceful imaginable. it is simply this_ The petticoat is tied round the neck and the arms put through the pocket_ holes!!!
Pub Decr 9. 1795 by S W Fores No 50 Piccadilly the Corner of Sackville Street_ NB Folios of Caricatures lent out for the Evening

Constitutions Ready for all Occasions
Satans, return from ~~Egypt~~ Earth. Discoverd in Council — with Belzebub & Belial. —— a Sketch after Fuseli —!!!
feci
Publish'd Novr 30 1799 by S W Fores Piccadilly where

24.

John Cawse (1778–1862), designer; F. Sansom (*fl. c.*1797–1810), engraver

Satan's Return from ~~Egypt~~ Earth. Discovered in Council — with Belzebub & Belial — a Sketch after Fuseli — !!!

Lettered: 'Publishd Novr 30 1799 by SW Fores Piccadilly'

Hand-coloured etching, 353 x 268 mm

Literature: BM Satires 9431

This satire refers to Napoleon's surprise appearance in Paris in autumn 1799 after his return from his ill-fated Egyptian campaign. On 9 and 10 November he overthrew the Directory and established the Consulate, in which he became First Consul. Fores later amusingly described himself on his prints as 'caricaturist to the first consul'. The *coup d'état* that established the Consulate was carried out by Napoleon with the support of Pierre Roger Ducos (1747–1816) and the revolutionary, Abbé Emmanuel Joseph Sieyès (1748–1836), who, together with Napoleon, made up the first three consuls.

Here the three consuls are depicted as a Holy Trinity, underlined by the triangle of knives behind Napoleon's Head. Each side of the triangle has an inscription, 'Seyes' (left), 'Buonaparte' (right) and 'Ducos', while in the centre is the word 'Abbaye' (the prison where the September Massacres began). Bonaparte, head in hands, is seated on a throne in the clouds like Satan, the fallen angel. The subtitle of the satire – *A Sketch after Fuseli!!!* – refers to the Milton Gallery, which Henry Fuseli (1741–1825) opened in 1799 with forty-one paintings illustrating works by John Milton. Fuseli's image of Satan enthroned in Pandemonium, as in works like *Satan and the Birth of Sin* (*c.*1796–9; Dallas Museum of Art), provided the inspiration for satirising Napoleon as a Miltonic Satan. The tortured, miserable-looking Bonaparte is being looked at with apprehension by his fellow consuls and main supporters, depicted as the Miltonic Belzebub and Belial.

A host of little demons fly above them, in this case the English Jacobins Richard Sheridan, Michael Angelo Taylor (bap. 1757–1834) and Charles Stanhope (see cat.10). At the base of the print are Satan's dominions of devils, the revolutionary horde, who applaud their new master and wave *bonnets rouges* or daggers. One shouts 'Down with the Councils up wth the Committees', while another cries 'Vive La Babouf Ca ira'. The latter refers to the revolutionary, François-Noël Babeuf (1760–1797), who was executed, and 'Ca ira' (It'll be fine) was an emblematic song of the French Revolution.

25.

Isaac Cruikshank (1764–1811)

A Muddy, a Sketch in Bond Street!

Lettered: 'Pub April 3. 1800 by SW Fores, 50 Piccadilly'

Hand-coloured etching, 275 x 378 mm

Literature: James Peller Malcolm, *An Historical Sketch of the Art of Caricaturing*, London 1813, p.140

Mud was a problem in London and this print depicts it in Bond Street in 1800. In the background to the right can be seen a crossing sweeper, who cleared the way for pedestrians for whatever they would give. Like many at the time, he is a disabled military veteran who could probably find no other employment. He is shown in uniform and with one arm.

The main subject, as the title suggests, is centred around a carriage, or 'muddy'. Writing in 1813, James Peller Malcolm recorded the fashion of these coaches a decade earlier: 'It became the fashion, at the time this print was engraved, to build the coaches of people of rank so extremely low, and reduce the height of the wheels to such a degree, that the Caricaturist, in common with the publick, called them Muddys.' The carriage's small size and low position are emphasised by the large lackeys with their oversized clothes and hats. Spattered with mud, it pauses at the curb while the two ladies inside converse with two dandies on the pavement.

Pub April 3. 1800 by SW Fores. 50 Piccadilly
A MUDDY. a Sketch in Bond Street!!
Folios of Caricatures Lent

Is this the Gallant gay Lothario! Heavens how pale
Bless your heart my Lady no such a thing_dont you know me, I am my Lord Pic-Nic, one of the Dillitante Performers.
And I myself appear'd their leading God' theres an Alexcander the Great for you.
I will trouble you Ma am tothrow in a few more tears in the last passage.
In Vain with tears her loss she may deplore, In Vain look back, to what she was before, She sets like Stars that fall, to rise nomore.
O Pylades what's life without a freind!
You may call me Pylades orwhat you please, but I am determin'd to play nothing but Sir John Falstaff!!
A PEEP into TOTENHAM STREET or Dillitanti Performers in Training.

26.

Charles Williams (*fl.*1797–1830)

A Peep into Totenham Street or Dillitanti Performers in Training

Lettered: 'Pubd March 9th 1802 by S W Fores 50 Piccadilly'

Hand-coloured etching, 257 x 260 mm

Literature: BM Satires 9919

In 1802 Colonel Henry Francis Greville (born 1760) formed the Pic Nic Society, a group of amateur actors and actresses, who performed at a theatre on Tottenham Court Road. This amateur society threatened the professional theatres of London, and Richard Sheridan wrote to Greville on 17 February 1802, announcing his determination to oppose the society. There was great hostility to its formation. Their theatre was created in concert rooms developed by John Hyde in 1800 from an earlier 1770s building.

A number of satires caricatured their performances, including this by Charles Williams, who shows the oddly shaped and dressed society gesticulating in the most amateur manner during a rehearsal. The scene depicted evokes cacophony, overacting and the actors' delusion regarding their own abilities. A fat lady to the left, possibly Lady Buckinghamshire, exclaims with her left hand dramatically in the air: 'Is this the gallant gay Lothario! Heavens how pale.' An elderly gentleman looking through an eyeglass holding a huge muff, possibly the Duke of Queensbury, replies: 'Bless your heart my Lady no such a thing – dont you know me, I am my Lord Pic-Nic, one of the Dillitante Performers.'

27.

Charles Williams (*fl.*1797–1830)

A Trip to Paris or John Bull and his Spouse Invited to the Honors of the Sitting!!

Lettered: 'Pubd May 14th 1802 by S W Fores 50 Piccadilly'

Hand-coloured etching, 252 x 365 mm

Literature: BM Satires 9864; Broadley 1911, vol.1, p.155

On 25 March 1802 the Treaty of Amiens was signed as a 'Definitive Treaty of Peace' between the French and the British, although in reality it lasted only a year. This satire was produced shortly after the treaty was signed and depicts John Bull (Britain) and Hibernia (Ireland) visiting Napoleon in Paris. During the brief peace many visitors from Great Britain flocked to Paris.

Bonaparte sits at ease in his chair and is depicted without any caricature saying: 'Indeed Mr Bull I am quite charmed with you – there is something so easy and polite in Your manners.' John Bull and Hibernia are depicted as common and fat, made awkward by the honour of visiting Napoleon. John Bull sits uncomfortably holding his knees in a stiff position, while Hibernia scolds him in her pretension to gentility. John Bull says 'Come – come Mounseer Bonney-party that's all gammon d'ye see – D—n me if I know any more about politeness than a Cow does of a new shilling!!' Hibernia, who is John's wife through the Union, tries to act genteel by putting down the crudeness of her husband: 'For shame Mr Bull – what will the Jontleman think of your Blarney about Gammon and Cows, and Bodder, and Nonsense, by St Patrick I must send You to Kilkenny to larn good breeding.' The caricature mocks the sudden fascination and admiration for France and the French, doubting the sincerity of Bonaparte in his new-found cordiality with the British.

Indeed Mr Bull I am quite charmed with you—there is something so easy and polite in Your manners.
Come-come Mounseer Bony thats all gammon d'ye see-D—n me if I know any more about politeness than a Cow does of a new shilling!!
For shame Mr Bull-what will the Jontleman think of your Blarney about Gammon and Cows, and Bodder and Nonsense, by St Patrick, I must send You to Kilkenny to larn good breeding.
A TRIP to PARIS or JOHN BULL and his SPOUSE invited to the Honors of the SITTING!!

Eh you Bull Dog, val you carry off dat Bone for, I vas come to take dat myself. I vas good mind to lick you, but for dem Dam Tooths.
There Monkey, that for you
MALTA
JOHN BULL
ENGLAND
Plan for Ingadeing England
Pub^d June 14th 1803 by S W Fores N° 50 Piccadilly
THE BONE of CONTENTION or the English Bull Dog and the Corsican Monkey
Folios of Caricatures lent out for the Evening

28.

Charles Williams (*fl.*1797–1830)

The Bone of Contention or the English Bull Dog and the Corsican Monkey

Lettered: 'Pubd June 14th 1803 by S W Fores No 50 Piccadilly'

Hand-coloured etching, 246 x 352 mm

Literature: BM Satires 10015

On 25 March 1802 the Treaty of Amiens temporarily ended hostilities between the French Republic and Great Britain. The peace was only brief, lasting one year. One of the main reasons for the failure of the treaty was Britain's refusal to remove troops from Malta, which it had deployed when defeating the French occupation there in 1800. Britain declared war on France on 18 May 1803 as a result of France's aggressive imperialist policies, thus beginning the Napoleonic Wars that would rage in Europe for over a decade. Following the declaration of war, Napoleon planned an invasion of Britain building huge flotillas of flat-bottomed boats, while Britain prepared its defences.

It is against this background that this satire was created, depicting Napoleon as a Corsican Monkey frustrated by the English bulldog. Both stand on a map, the French part of which is entitled 'Plan for Invadeing England'. The bulldog stands on England and urinates into the English Channel onto the invasion plans of Bonaparte, saying: 'There Monkey, that for you.' In his mouth is a huge bone inscribed 'MALTA', the bone of contention between Britain and France. The Monkey stands on the map of France on top of a long list of invasion craft ('flat bottom boats') with both hands extended, exclaiming: 'Eh you Bull Dog, vat you carry off dat Bone for, I vas come to take dat myself, I vas good mind to lick you, but for dem Dam Tooths.'

29.

Isaac (1764–1811) and George (1792–1878) Cruikshank

French Generals Receiving an English Charge

Lettered: 'Pubd. by SW Fores 50 Piccadilly April 28th 1809'

Hand-coloured etching, 236 x 336 mm

Literature: BM Satires 11322

Talleyrand, Napoleon and his generals are greatly amused, it seems, by English caricatures (*charges* in French). Seated on a throne, Napoleon shows Talleyrand his Isaac Cruikshank print, *Military Leap Frog or Hints to Young Gentlemen by Messrs Blackwood & Co*, published by Fores on 5 June 1807 (BM Satires 10740) and depicting Mrs Clarke receiving bribes for military promotions. 'Aye, Tally,' Napoleon says, 'this is not the way I reward Merit by putting inexperienced Boys over the Heads of experienced Veterans.' The other prints enjoyed by the generals are *Mrs Clarke's Petticoat* (23 February 1809; BM Satires 11220), *Raising the Wind* (17 March 1809; BM Satires 11257) and *Church Promotion, or How to Scale a Pulpit!* (25 February 1809; BM Satires 11224); and *An Irish Introduction to a Royal Pulpit* (16 March 1809; BM Satires 11255) is on the table. All the prints are published by Fores and depict the Duke of York and the corruption of his mistress, Mrs Clarke (see cat.30), who sold positions for money and as favours to lovers.

Napoleon, Talleyrand and his generals present amusing caricatures, particularly Bonaparte with his enormous bicorne hat, boots up to the thighs and massive spurs. The real target, however, was the Duke of York, commander-in-chief of the British army, who is being mocked by his enemy. 'Dere is nothing to be feared from such Petticoat Commanders', laughs one general. It is also interesting to see the portrayal of exported English satirical prints, which were widespread in Europe, although London was by far the largest market. Even though this is an imagined scene, it is clear that these prints caused amusement in France.

FRENCH GENERALS receiving an English CHARGE.

" Altho I dont keep a Barouche of my own,
" I've a fine stud of Asses and they're all the Ton., Come up Neddy's.
Now you shall see how I manage my Ponies, I can turn them as easy as I can myself the leader Fred I have been flogging lately, & he has taken to kick this poor Devil Gwilly most unmercifully I have but lately brore him into the Shafts.
Aye Aye. you have done Wright
Come up Dowley! I hope I shall soon be admitted to a more favored situation, I have been in waiting long enough
KINGS ROAD
Pub.d July 10th 1809 by S.W. Fores 50 Piccadilly
Mrs CLARKE DRIVING her PONIES. Vide Chapter of Donkies. If it was'nt for Asses pray what would she do. vers: 5th.

30.

Charles Williams (*fl.*1797–1830)

Mrs Clarke Driving her Ponies

Lettered: 'Pubd July 10th 1809 by S.W. Fores 50 Piccadilly'

Hand-coloured etching, 256 x 369 mm

Literature: BM Satires 11345

Mary Anne Clarke (1776?–1852) was the mistress of Frederick, Duke of York (1763–1827), between 1803 and 1806. At the beginning of the affair Mrs Clarke, with the Duke of York's patronage, took a large house in Gloucester Place, where she entertained on an extravagant scale. She also made further money from the affair by using her lover's position as commander-in-chief, promising promotion to officers, in return for payment. On 27 January 1809 Colonel Gwyllym Lloyd Wardle (1761/2–1833) raised the matter in the House of Commons, and an investigation into corruption took place between 1 February and 20 March. Although the committee accepted that it was a careless episode on the part of the duke, they could find no evidence of his receiving money from the transactions and no grounds for prosecution. The duke did resign as commander-in-chief, however, and the scandal was widely satirised.

The government found an opportunity to attack Wardle later in the year when an upholsterer, Francis Wright, took an action against him for not paying for the furnishings of Mrs Clarke's residence. It emerged that these decorations were a payment for her help in bringing his case against the duke, and the jury found against Wardle. This caricature, subtitled 'If it was'nt for Asses pray what would she do', satirises the action against Wardle. It depicts Mrs Clarke in the driving seat whipping two donkeys with the heads of the Duke of York ('Fred') and Wardle ('Gwilly'). Donkey Fred is violently kicking donkey Gwilly, as Mrs Clarke exclaims:

> Come up Neddy's. Now you shall see how I manage my Ponies. I can turn them as easy as I can myself the leader Fred I have been flogging lately, & he has taken to kick this poor Devil Gwilly most unmercifully I have but lately brore [*sic*] him into the Shafts.

Beside her sits Wright, the upholsterer, with a bill for the work he has done on her residence. Behind the cart is Captain William Dowler, who declares: 'Come up Dowley! I hope I shall soon be admitted to a more favored situation; I have been in waiting long enough.' Dowler was a lover of Mrs Clarke and for a time she passed as his wife.

31.

William Heath (1794–1840)

The Taylor Sheering the Geese or the Protestants in the Wrong Box

Lettered: 'Pub Feb 8th 1811 by Fores 50 Picadilli'

Hand-coloured etching, 243 x 349 mm

Literature: BM Satires 11766

This is a satire of the opera at the King's Theatre, Haymarket, when it was under the management of Mr William Taylor (*c.*1753–1825). As one critic wrote two months before this satire was published, the theatre is 'in the hands of a manager so destitute of taste and liberality … The talents most esteemed by him [Taylor] are those that be procured for the least money' (H.R., *The Examiner*, 10 Dec. 1810). Whether the main figure, who is a tailor, is William Taylor or not (he was in his late fifties in 1811) is uncertain, but it is clear that the satire is directed at his management of the theatre.

Here the manager is shown snipping at the dresses of young ladies, revealing their buttocks, and driving them away, as the boxes are all full. He shouts: 'If I have not a right to do as I will with my own, who has, if you conspire to injure me I will Clip you depend on it So off off¡¡¡' The second part of the title, 'the Protestants in the Wrong Box', refers to the call, ignored by Taylor, to have more operas performed in English (i.e. for the Protestants) rather than Italian. Taylor was a controversial figure who was bankrupted and lived a great deal of his life in debtors' prison. The dress of the tailor is unkempt and down at heel indicating the poverty and disrepair of the theatre, which was widely commented on at the time.

BOXES all TAKEN
If I have not a right to do as I will with my own, who has. if you conspire to injure me I will clip you depend on it So off off !!!
upon my life he handles his Yard Famously
aye and Sheers too I think,
THE TAYLOR-SHEERING the GEESE or the Protestants in the wrong Box

ELBA BABEL
Ah Diable Mai you was burn Le Matereiel, you burn your playtings
Now these fellows shall know what the Conqueror of the World can do
Corporal! D— you Sir, dont you blow up the Bridge till I order you
BONEY at ELBA or a Madman's Amusement.
"So high he's mounted in his airy Throne,
"That now the wind is got into his Head,
"And turns his brain to Frenzy. —— Dryden
Pubd April 20th 1814 by S.W. Fores No 50 Piccadilly

32.

Charles Williams (*fl.*1797–1830)

Boney at Elba or a Madman's Amusement

Lettered: 'Pubd April 20th 1814 by S.W. Fores No 50 Piccadilly'

Hand-coloured etching, 247 x 352 mm

Literature: BM Satires 12229

On 11 April 1814 the Treaty of Fontainebleau was signed, and according to its conditions, the Emperor Napoleon had to abdicate and go into exile on the Tuscan island of Elba. Bonaparte arrived at Portoferraio, Elba, on 30 May 1814 to begin his exile. Although he was allowed a large personal guard of several hundred men, the island was patrolled by the British Royal Navy. This satire, published on the day Napoleon left Fontainebleau for the island, imagines him as a crazed and deluded despot who sees himself as 'Conqueror of the World'.

The demented Napoleon has made himself a crown and sceptre of straw. He is igniting a canon, also made of straw, which immediately catches fire, prompting a French soldier to cry: 'Ah Diable Mai you was burn Le Matereiel, you burn your playtings.' The canon is aimed at four straw figures representing in turn: Alexander of Russia, wearing the emblem of a bear; Frederick William III of Prussia, wearing the emblem of a Hohenzollern eagle; Francis I of Austria, wearing the emblem of a Habsburg eagle; and Bernadotte of Sweden, wearing the emblem of a cross. Bonaparte calls out: 'Now these fellows shall know what the Conqueror of the World can do! Corporal? D— you Sir! don't you blow up the Bridge till I order you.' On the ground, by the abdicated emperor's feet, are papers that reflect his lunatic megalomania: 'Project to Invade the Moon' and 'Grant of the Senate 6,000,000'.

33.

Charles Williams (*fl.*1797–1830)

The Cream of the Joke or Boney's Last Bulletin

Lettered: 'Pubd May 2d 1814 by S W Fores 50 Piccadilly, where may be had all the Carricature of Bonaparte's life'

Hand-coloured etching, 250 x 355 mm

Literature: BM Satires 12257

This satire was produced at the time that Napoleon was travelling from Fontainebleau to Elba between 20 April and 30 May 1814. It depicts the abdicated emperor with his hands tied behind his back riding his famous white horse, Marengo (*c.*1793–1831), looking very skinny and tired. He is followed by a group of Cossacks, the front two of whom are prodding Bonaparte and his horse with their spears. He is dictating a bulletin to a French officer, who writes on a long roll of paper that stretches out into a coil on the ground.

Napoleon says: 'Tell the Lads of Paris – I have taken two thousand of the D—d Cossack's, and am going to transport them to the Island of Elba!!!' The French officer answers: 'Mais Sire! Ces Diables des Cossak's your prisoners – take the liberty of the Master and wont let you tell de lie any more!' The front cossacks say: 'Come! Come! push on the Lads of Paris are not to be hum'd any longer!' and 'Aye! stop till we lodge you in El-bay and then you and the old one may try which can lie fastest.' The island of Elba can be seen in the far left of the image.

Mais Sire! ces diables des Cossak's your prisoners — take the liberty of the Master and wont let you tell de lie any more! —
Tell the Lads of Paris — I have taken two thousand of the D—d Cossack's, and am going to transport them to the Island of Elba !!! ——
Come! Come! push on the Lads of Paris are not to be humm'd any longer! —
Aye! stop till we lodge you in El-bay and then you and the old one may try which can lie fastest . —
Abdication
THE CREAM of the JOKE or Boney's last Bulletin.
"Boasters are naturally falsifiers, and the "people of all others, that put their shams the worst together. — L'Estrange's Fables.
Pubd. May 2d. 1814 by S W Fores 50 Piccadilly, where may be had all the Caricatures of Bonaparte's life

Courage my dearest Princess, trust in GOD & all will be well
Is there any danger?
GCk
Pub.d by S W Fores 50 Piccadilly Dec.r 2.d 1817
Englands ONLY Hope Departing
A Specimen of Conjugal affection & attention in Exalted life — a Lesson to Princes

34.

George Cruikshank (1792–1878)

Englands Only Hope Departing

Lettered: 'Pubd. by S W Fores 50 Piccadilly Decr. 2d. 1817'

Hand-coloured etching, 273 x 382 mm

Literature: BM Satires 12894

Princess Charlotte Augusta of Wales (1796–1817) died at 2.30 in the morning on 6 November 1817 five hours after the birth of a stillborn child. *The Times* reported: 'Prince Leopold was with her Royal Highness at this agonizing moment' (*The Times*, 7 Nov. 1817, p.2). This tragic event of royal history caused a wave of national grief. Widely referred to as England's Hope, she was a contrast to her disliked father and grandfather, who was thought mad. Had she survived, she would have succeeded to the throne. The Whigs, who had championed the princess with the wider public, lost a future hope. She was buried at St George's Chapel, Windsor, on 19 November 1817.

The scene depicted shows Princess Charlotte on her deathbed asking Prince Leopold, who is on his knees beside her: 'Is there any danger?' The Prince replies: 'Courage my dearest Princess, trust in God & all will be well.'

35.

Henry Heath (*fl.*1822–1842)

The Wits of Windsor, a Milton-ian Pun

Lettered: 'Pubd Septr. 10, 1827 by S W Fores, 41 Piccadilly, London'

Hand-coloured etching, 236 x 372 mm

This satire on coach travel shows two coaches from London to Windsor racing each other. The coachman of the coach behind, which is being passed, complains: 'I'm the Regulator Mat.' The coachman of the passing coach shouts back: 'Yes, we know it Jack for we all Go by you.'

The joke is that the Regulator sets the time for the journey, which is clearly slow, as the 'go by you' has the pun or double meaning of setting the time as well as passing by.

I'm the Regulator Mat.
Yes we know it Jack for we all Go by you.
J. MOODY
WINDSOR
CORONET
ETON
WINDSOR
LONDON
SLOUGH
WINDSOR
THE WITS OF WINDSOR. a Milton-ian Pun.

36.

Anonymous

Installation of the New Deputy Grand Master of the Most Veritable Order of the Red Halter

Lettered: 'London pubd by S.W. Fores 41 Picadilly Septr 12 1827'

Hand-coloured etching, 225 x 326 mm

Literature: BM Satires 15422

As indicated in the reference after the title, the editions of the '*Morning Post* July 10th & 19th 1827' provided the basis of this satire, although its source had remained elusive. Page 2 of each of these editions contains a full satire of Brougham and his colleagues by 'A Constitutional Whig', including the comic scene at the centre of this caricature. The target was Brougham's personal ambition, his rebellion and the forming of a coalition in 1827. Interestingly on p.3 of the *Morning Post* of 10 July an article entitled 'Mr Brougham' highlights the personal ambition of Henry Peter Brougham (1778–1868; see cat.37), stating: 'He was not satisfied with a mere silk gown in the general promotion.' The article is prefaced:

> To the Editor of the Morning Post
>
> Sir– Having been exclusively favoured with the Ceremonial to be observed upon the Installation of the Knights of 'The Most Veritable Order of the Red Halter,' together with some preparatory proceedings, I hasten to transcribe the most material parts of both for the information of those of your Readers who delight in heraldry; And I remain, Sir, &c. A CONSTITUTIONAL WHIG

The scene is then described, consisting of a ceremonial dinner led by Grand Master Brougham with his Deputy Canning (George Canning, 1770–1827, who was in fact prime minister at the time):

> The Halter King at Arms had superintended the erection of the stalls in the Hall of the Cockney University, and also a brazen pulpit in the middle of it, round which tables were formed, till there was large enough to dine the Knights and Officers … The Twelve Knights, the four Assistants to the Master, and *Sir John Ketch*, appeared in full costume; the others carried the red or crimson silk mantles [halters] upon the left arm, and their helmets in the right hand.

Here the central pulpit is inscribed 'Taylor's Pillar', referring to the heretical Robert Taylor (1784–1844), who preached deistical sermons in episcopal dress and was charged with blasphemy. He is shown from the back holding a Bible in a pair of shears, saying: 'I am their Bishop and Consience Keeper.' The *Morning Post* describes 'The Dean', who 'ascended the pulpit, and preached for two hours to the Knights a sermon which no one could understand a word of … No Bible here, remember you are in the Cockney University.'

Around the pulpit is a horseshoe-shaped table where the dinner is taking place. The only drink available is porter, a barrel of which can be seen, accompanied by William Henry Whitbread (1795–1867), the brewer and politician. As in numerous satires, Brougham is holding a broom and standing on 'his State Chair of brass' (*Morning Post*, 10 or 19 July 1827, p.2). Holding a frothing pint of porter, he exclaims: 'I did all I could for you, but don't interrupt me & the Noble Champion at this important Crisis!!' The 'noble champion' to whom he refers is the figure on the horse, as the *Morning Post* describes: 'The Noble Champion then entered, clad in brass from head to foot, and sitting upon a large wooden horse (there was no living horse strong enough).' Looking like Don Quixote with an enormous lance and spurs, he stands in his stirrups and says: 'I am ready at your call, to Challenge all, both great and small, but not Small Beer.'

To the right of the champion is a figure inscribed 'Sir J. Ketch', the proverbial name of an executioner, so in this case holding the halter or noose. (John Ketch, generally known as Jack Ketch, who died in November 1686, was an infamous English executioner employed by King Charles II.) He says: 'If they're hopstropilous turn them over to me.' Behind the table to the right of the pillar a figure in blue raises a gridiron and shouts: 'I'll rattle the Rogues over my Gridiron.' This is William Cobbett (1763–1835), political writer and farmer, who famously declared that he would roast himself on a gridiron if the government could achieve what they claimed on the national debt, and as a result his critics included sketches of gridirons in their writings and cartoons of him.

Seated at the front in the centre is Sir Francis Burdett, 5th Baronet (1770–1844). To the left of him is William George Spencer Cavendish, 6th Duke of Devonshire (1790–1858), a Whig grandee and connoisseur of the arts who served as Lord Chamberlain to both George IV (in 1827–8) and William IV (in 1830–34). Just behind him is Sir Matthew Wood, 1st Baronet (1768–1843), a druggist and politician, here holding a tankard inscribed 'Sir absolute'. Behind the cask is Henry Petty-Fitzmaurice, 3rd Marquess of Lansdowne (1780–1863), who says: 'When I consented to succeed Cang [Canning] as Deputy grand, I was also to succeed him as Premier – I have not been well treated!!'

Other figures referred to in the *Morning Post* were part of the political upheaval of 1827, and possibly also represented here are Sir Henry Hunt, Sir George Warrender, Lord Holland, Sir Robert Wilson, Earl Grey and Sir John Stevenson.

37.

H. Heath (*fl.*1822–1842)

A Hasty Stride from Broom Hall to West Mstr Hall

Lettered: 'Pubd 1830. by. S.W. Fores. 41 Piccadilly, London'

Hand-coloured etching, 251 x 357 mm

Literature: BM Satires 16349

In 1830 Henry Peter Brougham (1778–1868), after resigning his seat in Winchester, stood for Yorkshire, where he campaigned tirelessly as the outside candidate and won the campaign. In search of political reform, he endangered the stability of the government, so was offered the role of Lord Chancellor, and on 22 November 1830 he received the great seal and was ennobled the next day as first Baron Brougham and Vaux.

This satire depicts Brougham in the formal dress of a Lord Chancellor with wig and black gown leaping from the House of Commons to the House of Lords. On the right his Yorkshire constituents are saying: 'A pretty fellow to leave his Constituents!' As he leaps over the lords, they look up exclaiming 'Did you ever see such a Jump?' The caricature plays on Brougham's pursuit of personal ambition over loyalty to his constituents and the remarkable speed with which he moved from election in Yorkshire to taking up position as Lord Chancellor.

Whatever Ministry his Majesty may choose will not affect me!!!
Sic itur ad Astra and leave the world beneath
A pretty fellow to leave his Constituents!
Did you ever see such a Jump?
DROIT
YORK
Pub.d 1830, by S.W. Fores, 41 Piccadilly London.
H. Heath fect.
A HASTY STRIDE, from BROOM HALL - to WEST.mstr HALL!

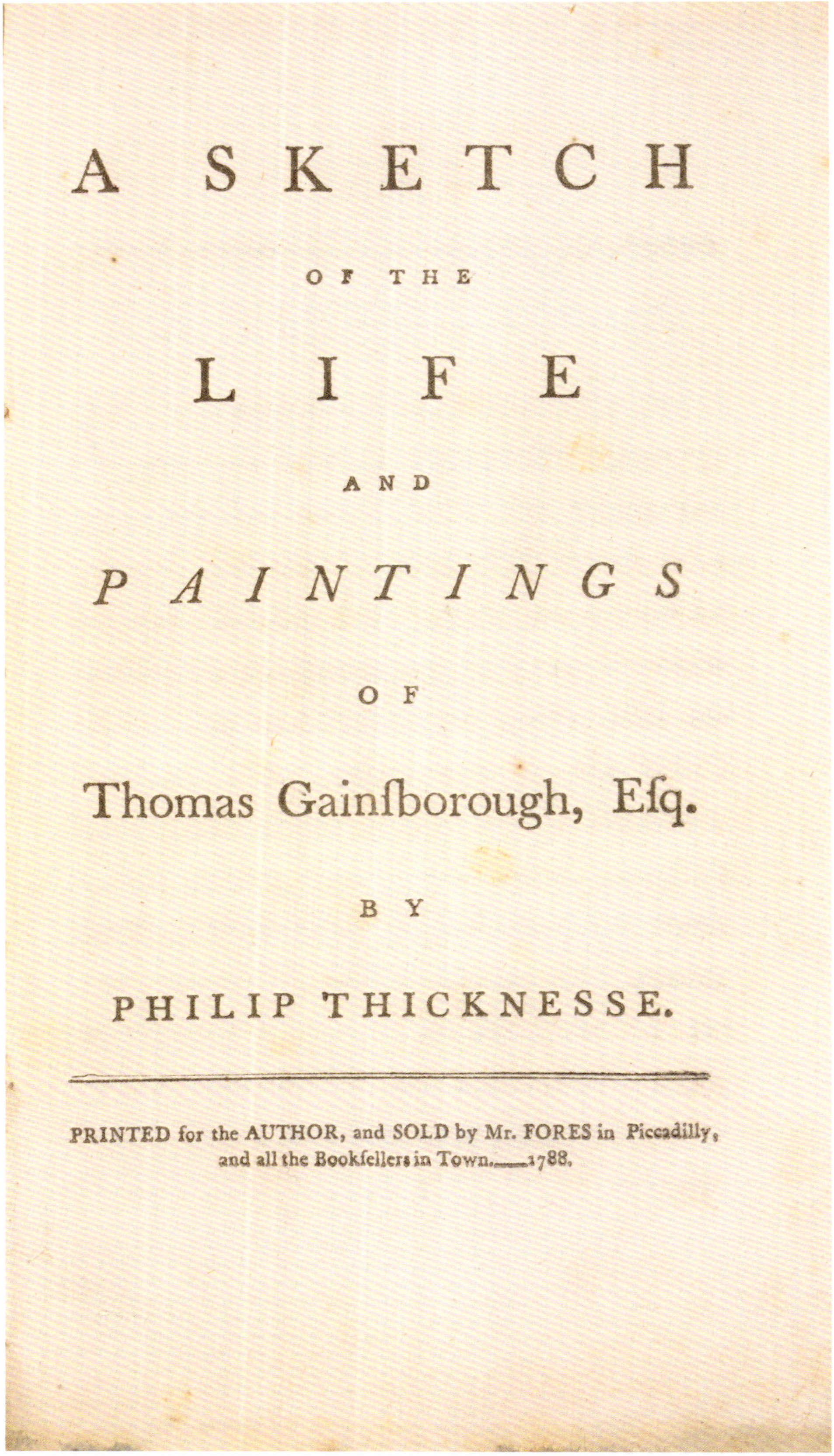

A SKETCH

OF THE

LIFE

AND

PAINTINGS

OF

Thomas Gainſborough, Eſq.

BY

PHILIP THICKNESSE.

PRINTED for the AUTHOR, and SOLD by Mr. FORES in Piccadilly, and all the Bookſellers in Town.——1788.

38.

Philip Thicknesse (1719–1792)

A Sketch of the Life and Paintings of Thomas Gainsborough, Esq. By Philip Thicknesse

Published by S.W. Fores, London, 1788

Fores was a friend of Philip Thicknesse and was involved in a number of projects with him. These included publications and the loan of exhibition items, most famously the wax head and hand of the unfortunate Count Struensee (see pp.19–20). Thicknesse had known Thomas Gainsborough and the Gainsborough family since the 1750s and gave Fores a steam-engine model made by Humphrey Gainsborough (1718–1776, an older brother of Thomas Gainsborough); Fores described this as 'much decayed and disordered by being exposed to the weather by his brother in Pall Mall' (11 March 1785, Boulton and Watt Collection, Birmingham City Archive), where Thomas Gainsborough had his studio at Schomberg House. Thomas Gainsborough died in 1788 and Thicknesse worked with Fores to have this, the first printed biography of the artist, published shortly after the artist's death.

Chronology

1737 Birth of Samuel Fores, father of S.W. Fores

1760 Samuel Fores marries Mary Allington

1761 Samuel William Fores born on 8 March and baptised on 29 March at St Benet Fink, Threadneedle Street, London

1770s Samuel Fores is listed as operating a bookshop at no.120 Strand

1775 12 May: apprenticed to his father for a term of seven years

1782 His apprenticeship ends

***c*.1782** William Holland (his main competitor) begins his caricature business

1783 Opens a caricature print shop at the City Arms, no.3 Piccadilly, near Haymarket

Marries Elizabeth Green (1758–1797)

William Pitt the Younger becomes prime minister at the age of twenty-four

1784 January: Fores prints his first caricatures

Birth of daughter Elizabeth

Votes Tory in the Westminster elections

1785 Birth of son Samuel William Dakin

1787 June: opens a caricature exhibition at his shop at no.3 Piccadilly

Birth of son Phillip Henry

1788 Votes Tory in the Westminster elections

26 June: signs a contract with James Gillray to produce a serious portrait of Willam Pitt

Publishes *A Sketch of the Life and Paintings of Thomas Gainsborough, Esq.* by Philip Thicknesse

William Holland opens his caricature exhibition

1789 Advertises as the largest caricature exhibition in the kingdom, 'forming an entire Caricature History, political and domestic, of past and present Times'

14 July: French Revolution begins with the storming of the Bastille. Charles James Fox, Opposition Whig leader, declares: 'How much the greatest event that has happened in the history of the world, and how much the best'

Publishes Gillray's portrait of William Pitt and falls out with the artist over it

Authentic Elucidation of the History of Counts Struensee and Brandt (translated from the German) published

1790 Birth of son Charles

June: puts the wax head and hand of Count Struensee on display until May 1793

Briefly reconciled with James Gillray, who produces some prints for him this year

1792 Birth of daughter Anna Maria

September Massacres in Paris

1793 21 January: Louis XVI executed by guillotine

1 February: revolutionary France declares war against Great Britain and Holland

March: Sets up a 6ft model of a guillotine in his shop

Publishes *Man-midwifery dissected; or, the obstetric family-instructor … In fourteen letters. Addressed to A. Hamilton …* by John Blunt

1795 Birth of son Henry Philip

Moves to no.50 Piccadilly at the corner of Sackville Street and Piccadilly

1796 23 January: Gillray is arrested, along with Fores and other printsellers, charged with selling Gillray's *The Presentation – or – The Wise Mens Offering*, which depicts the birth of Princess Charlotte

12 March: *The True Briton* newspaper announces: 'We are happy to find that our strictures on the scandalous caricature-exhibitions ... have had the desired effect. Humour has taken the place of Licentiousness and the works of Genius are substituted for the Fruits of Sedition.'

Birth of son Richard A.

1797 Birth of son Frederick William

Death of his wife Elizabeth

1799 He is robbed at home in Piccadilly

Napoleon overthrows the Directory and establishes the Consulate, becoming First Consul

*c.***1800** Marries Jane Blucher (1772–1840)

The Duke of Orléans, Louis-Philippe (1773–1850), arrives in England and stays with Fores over his shop in Piccadilly

1801 Birth of daughter Emma

1802 Takes Thomas Johnes MP (1748–1816) to court for failure to pay for over 1,000 caricature prints

25 March: Treaty of Amiens temporarily ends hostilities between the French Republic and Great Britain

1803 18 May: Great Britain declares war on France

1804 Birth of daughter Jane Amelia

1804 Birth of daughter Maria

1805 Birth of son Horatio

1806 Birth of son George Thomas

1809 Birth of daughter Helen Lavinia

1814 Birth of son Arthur Blücher

11 April: Treaty of Fontainebleau is signed, forcing Napoleon's abdication and exile to the Tuscan island of Elba

1815 26 February: Napoleon escapes from Elba

18 June: Napoleon defeated at Waterloo

*c.***1815** Roxburgh Collection of Caricatures advertised as twenty-four volumes at 250 guineas

1816 Birth of daughter Harriet Sophia

1818–19 He also has premises at no.312 Oxford Street

*c.***1820** Street numbers change so that no.50 becomes no.41 Piccadilly

1821 Edward Everett charged with gross improprieties outside Fores's shop

5 May: Napoleon dies on the remote South Atlantic island of Saint Helena

1825 John Grossett Muirhead accused of gross improprieties outside his shop and Fores gives evidence

1837 Votes Liberal in the Westminster elections

1838 Dies on 3 February and is buried in the Fores family vault at St James's, Piccadilly. The business continues to be run by his sons George Thomas Fores and Arthur Blücher Fores, who turn to sporting prints.

Select Bibliography

Alexander 1998
David Alexander, *Richard Newton and English Caricature in the 1790s*, Manchester University Press 1998

Angelo 1828–30
Henry Angelo, *Reminiscences of Henry Angelo, with Memoirs of his Late Father and Friends ...*, 2 vols, London 1828–30

Anon. 1912
Anon., 'The Firm and its Story, IV Fores, 41, Piccadilly', *Fine Art Trade Journal*, Nov. 1912, pp.387–90

Bindman 1989
David Bindman, *The Shadow of the Guillotine: Britain and the French Revolution*, London 1989

BM Satires
M. Dorothy George, *Catalogue of Political and Personal Satires Preserved ... in the British Museum*, vols 5–11, London 1935–54

Broadley 1911
Alexander Meyrick Broadley, *Napoleon in Caricature, 1795–1821*, 2 vols, London 1911

Donald 1996
Diana Donald, *The Age of Caricature: Satirical Prints in the Reign of George III*, New Haven 1996

Godfrey 2001
Richard T. Godfrey, *James Gillray: The Art of Caricature*, London 2001

Hill 1965
Draper Hill, *Mr Gillray the Caricaturist: A Biography*, London 1965

Kremers 2014
Anorthe Kremers, ed., *Loyal Subversion?: Caricatures from the Personal Union between England and Hannover (1714–1837)*, Göttingen 2014

The Print Shop Window ~ Caricature & Visual Satire in the Long Eighteenth Century at http://theprintshopwindow.wordpress.com

Turner 2008
Simon Turner, 'Fores, Samuel William (bap. 1761, d. 1838)', *Oxford Dictionary of National Biography*, Oxford University Press, 2004; online edn, Jan. 2008 (http://www.oxforddnb.com/view/article/63093, accessed 29 Jan. 2014)

Archives

Prints and Drawings Department, British Museum, London

New York Public Library

Adelphi University, New York

Curzon Collection, Bodleian Library, University of Oxford